BASEMENT OF WOLVES

DANIEL ALLEN COX

ARSENAL PULP PRESS | VANCOUVER

ARSENAL PULP PRESS
#101-211 East Georgia St.
Vancouver, BC
Canada V6A 1Z6
arsenalpulp.com

The publisher gratefully acknowledges the support of the Canada Council for
the Arts and the British Columbia Arts Council for its publishing program, and
the Government of Canada (through the Book Publishing Industry Development
Program) and the Government of British Columbia (through the Book
Publishing Tax Credit Program) for its publishing activities.

This is a work of fiction. Any resemblance of characters to persons either living
or deceased is purely coincidental.

Editing by Susan Safyan
Author photograph by Dallas Curow, dallascurow.com
Photograph on the cover by Jordan Halsey, jordanhalsey.com

Printed and bound in Canada on 100% post-consumer recycled paper

Library and Archives Canada Cataloguing in Publication:

Cox, Daniel Allen
        Basement of wolves / Daniel Allen Cox.

Issued also in electronic formats.
ISBN 978-1-55152-446-7

        I. Title.

PS8605.O934B38 2012   C813'.6   C2012-900503-7

PRAISE FOR *KRAKOW MELT*:

"Cox's splintered narrative, polished to an incisive gloss, bristles with both mischief and menace, and any of its short, titled chapters could stand alone. References to Pink Floyd, Polish pope John Paul II, and an unquenchable anger course from the first page to the last—a pointillistic poisoned pill." —*Publishers Weekly*

"A strangely wonderful book, an incendiary tribute to outlawed desires." —*Montreal Mirror*

"Cox employs terse, effective prose to reveal the consciousness of his characters and the time in which they live. His ability to create an entire world view and a sense of place—in few pages—is exceptional. In this respect, his style recalls that of another talented gay writer, Jeanette Winterson." —*Bay Area Reporter*

"A beautifully subversive novel ... Cox is among the top young writers in this country. He is courageous, creative and inventive." —*Front&Centre*

PRAISE FOR *SHUCK*:

"An invigorating first novel ... Cox's New York City has an off-hand, vibrant authenticity. It glitters and fumes." —*The Globe and Mail*

"A startling debut novel ... A distinctive coming-of-age story that poses thoughtful questions about the relationship between sex work and the creative process. A novel worth reading—for writers, whores, and everyone in between." —*Quill and Quire*

"As *Shuck* draws to a close, the author subtly points to a rethinking of our culture's larger attitudes towards sex workers. That Cox manages to convey these larger ideas without heavy-handedness makes *Shuck* one of those rare books that has both ample brains and raunchy sex appeal." —*Gay and Lesbian Review*

"There's a safety in thinking in a diner. You can have your coffee or your milk shake, and you can go off into strange dark areas, and always come back to the safety of the diner."

—David Lynch, from *Catching the Big Fish*

For Kevin Killian

ACKNOWLEDGMENTS

Thank you to the following bright lights for your immense help
with the book:

Robert Ballantyne, Dallas Curow, Linda Field, Brian Francis, Cynara
Geissler, Mark Ambrose Harris, Kevin Killian, Brian Lam, Susan
Safyan, Sarah Schulman, Shyla Seller.

I am grateful to work with you.

To the gang at Arsenal Pulp Press: Your support has meant so much.
Congrats on forty years of publishing.

Cheers to all other co-conspirators.

DAC

1.

THE BEST THING ABOUT Fontana restaurant, aside from the designer umbrella lost and found, the Stevie Wonder playing on a loop, and the mercury-free seaweed, is that I can always get the table I want, which is directly under a portrait of Miss Piggy wrapped in a feather boa, who, I swear on her hot pink ass, blows me a kiss every time I go there.

I had just gotten the casting call of a lifetime, so we went out to celebrate. The rumour was that I just had to show up, and the part was mine. Because so little effort was apparently required, I had a fantasy of arriving wasted, barely able to make it through the door, nostrils two cocaine hallways with a menthol bite, reeking of Jägermeister and other assorted spirits, maybe the stink of a half-dozen gin and tonics, Jack and Cokes downed in wonderfully poor judgement. Some wine. Shiraz. Guaranteed to make me puke. But I would be far too exhausted for puking, so I'd simply crawl through the doorway past the finish line and an assistant would lay a contract in my hand. I'd look at it, blurry, happy, and pass out. Though I don't do coke, so chances are it wouldn't happen that way.

That didn't mean I couldn't go out and get wrecked. We had a great time celebrating. I didn't mind when a few fans approached me. I'm afraid of chance encounters with admirers, because they're usually a little off. But these were nice, so I gave them autographs. One young woman asked me to sign her cellphone with a magic marker. Funny how fans always seem to have the writing instrument handy.

"Um, I feel bad, though," I said.

"You feel bad about what?"

"Ruining such a nice phone."

"It's a piece of garbage. I can't believe this. You're worried about my phone? Holy shit. But I mean, wow. Just do it, I don't care."

"Really?"

I uncapped the marker but hesitated. I was feeling mischievous.

"Wait a minute ... You want me to sign a phone you think is crappy? That's not much of a compliment."

"That's not what I meant."

"Why don't I wait until you get a new one? This is just going to end up in the trash."

"It's going to end up under my pillow. Fuck. That sounded so stupid."

"Ha ha, no worries."

Enough messing with her. I signed my name across the battery cover with a few rare flourishes I never do, loops and extended helixes, probably because of my great mood. Then I signed again right across the screen and keypad.

"My friends are never going to believe this," she said.

"Then let's make sure they do."

A crazy look came over her face: ready for adventure but afraid to ask for details. My friends were watching and listening, clearly enjoying the spectacle. I guess they don't often see me that happy, so it was probably a treat for them. I asked her to dial voicemail and navigate to the "record outgoing message" function, then I brought the phone to my lips and whispered into the receiver so she couldn't hear me over Stevie Wonder. I flipped the phone shut and wished her a good night.

The best part of this exchange was peering through the window and watching her check her outgoing message once she hit the sidewalk, my name pressed across her face and kissing it with a black stain, and then seeing her jump up and down. I hoped she was going to be a fan for life. The idea made me happy.

But my happiness is a veneer, a kind of makeup that pessimism always manages to wipe off by morning. That night, the negativity started with the creeping thought that there was always a way to lose a fan: just make a bad movie.

But I didn't have time for these mental storms, not with this party underway.

We had another few bottles of wine, *Grands Crus Bordeaux*, some fey custard and cream puff desserts that were just too much, and when we couldn't take any more we got up to pay and leave. The owner, Tony Fontana, put his hand on my shoulder and told me my card had been declined. Gasps all around. The loudest one came from me. Tony started laughing and told me to take it easy, that my card was fine. He was comping the meal to congratulate me on the audition I was supposedly going to ace. Then he warned me that if I managed to fuck it up, I owed him $6,000.

We left the restaurant and piled into our cars. My friend Steve got into my teal Porsche 944 and we took off east down Santa Monica Boulevard. I admit I was drunk, but at least in L.A. there are no pedestrians to hit, so my conscience got a free ride that night. Steve was tinkering with the GPS, reprogramming it to say impossible things, like turn left into this building, or turn around and continue straight for sixty miles, which would have sunk us into the ocean, and we were in such a good mood we actually considered going for a late-night shark swim.

We drove to Los Feliz and ended up at our usual club, an open-air terrace behind a crumbling brick façade, a holding pen for fashionistas who don't mind paying thirty bucks for a watery cocktail while they wait to be allowed on the dance floor, five at a time. We didn't have to wait or pay, but I felt bad butting in ahead of all the well-dressed queers. They were trying to start a new scene, my tribe, for sure. Maybe I was just drunk, but I couldn't take my eyes off this one young man wearing a pair of coke-bottle glasses. A collage of frames cut in half went up his forehead, like you were watching him take off his glasses in slow motion. A chill shook me. I might have been looking at the next Michael Alig, king of the Club Kids, version 3.0.

Nice White Teeth was in the VIP lounge drinking Jack and Coke. My friends and I hung out nearby and got sloshed on gin and tonics. I wanted to approach Nice White Teeth but was too shy. My friends joked about how he was probably a bigger fan of me than I was of him. Was I that famous? In a gentle, joking way they told me not to be stupid.

We sat on the circular red plush sofa, which miraculously didn't have a single stain on it, even after we got into heavy drinking that included Black Russians, and we started singing to the dated Gwen Stefani dance tracks, louder and louder, tanked and tipping, more in tune every passing minute, until finally I had to get up to piss. I continued singing on the way to the bathroom and well into letting out a diluted stream of cocktail mixers into the urinal, until my favourite Red Hot Chili Pepper pulled up beside me for a simultaneous whiz. At first, I thought I was daydreaming, but then I looked down and saw my dick, and understood how real it all was.

"You have quite the voice," Nice White Teeth said.

"Ha, thanks. But you're crazy."

"No, really. I mean it. You should come to the studio one day, and we'll record a backing vocal. We're always working on new stuff."

"Wow. That's cool. It's my birthday, you know. I'm forty."

I turned to look at his face, which was probably too intimate a gesture to pull in the bathroom, but by that point I had lost all control of the evening. It was going to unravel as it would.

"You shouldn't tell people that," Nice White Teeth said, as he zipped up and flushed.

"Why not?"

He left without answering my question. I decided on the spot, as drunk men missing the urinal and pissing on the tiled wall will sometimes do, that I couldn't listen to the albums of someone with such poor judgment in backing vocals anymore. I thought about what he said the whole drive home, and in bed alone trying to get the ceiling to stop spinning. And how could his teeth be even nicer than the lead singer's? I tried to clear my mind. I badly needed sleep so I could be sober for the audition, for the role I was guaranteed to land, even though I didn't believe in the rumour as fervently as everybody else did.

The next morning, I had a breakfast of ginseng and wheatgrass juice to erase the effects of the previous night's bender. I arrived at the studio sharp and alert, even looking pretty snappy in a cream tweed suit from DSquared2. Nothing too fancy, since I didn't want to seem presumptuous. I was feeling good, with no post-alcohol lows, dehydrated lips and tongue, or black bags under my eyes. On top of that, I got there an hour early, somehow missing the freeway traffic. I had been rehearsing my lines for weeks, exploring the cracks in the character's psyche. I felt like I had gotten a real sense of him, so I was relaxed.

The only problem was that Pinchable Cheeks was there.

You could say, if you wanted to find a lazy explanation, that my problems started with him. I certainly didn't know it at the time, but

I did feel the coldness, the shadow, the cloud, the coming changes in my life when we met that day.

I admired Pinchable Cheeks. He knew how to act, but also how to play the game; he had the fearlessness to treat his art as a business when necessary. Pinchable Cheeks exuded a sense of honesty; he seemed a plainspoken and straightforward Brooklyn kid who was awkward but still tough. This helped him stay popular with the indie crowd in New York, the Harvey Weinsteins, the Angelika Film Center buffs who scoffed if you defiled art house cinema by asking for a bag of popcorn. But he was also a hunk and could turn on the smoulder, that look in the eye that makes everybody wet these days, boy, Pinchable Cheeks had it, just delivered it straight into the camera like nicotine into the bloodstream, and this is what kept him popular in Hollywood. I wonder if people saw him as a new James Dean, if hope made them imagine him driving late one night in the hills, our hills, then swerving too late around a corner, a hot crash of melting steel to seal him into rock, pavement, and immortality. Yes, that's the effect Pinchable Cheeks had out here, and that's why I hated his guts. It's extremely rare to be popular on both coasts, not to mention Sundance and Toronto. The four locales offered him a continuous flow of jobs, hoping he'd pick a favourite. Of course, he never did, because that's not how the game is played.

I found out that Pinchable Cheeks and I were supposed to run through a scene together. I assumed we were competing for the same part. Where was the Achilles heel on a new, mid-thirties James Dean? I could only wonder, because it didn't show on any of his exposed skin.

"What's up," Pinchable Cheeks said.

"Hey."

"Your last movie was great."

I wondered if he knew how much I hated the word "movie." To me, it's what a piece of celluloid is called when it fails to be a film. A film is art. A movie is a background of light and noise to soothe people through a physical abuse session of stuffing their faces with candy.

"I didn't know you got out and saw stuff," I replied.

"Well, I didn't *see* it per se, but I heard it was fantastic. And I just wanted to say, no hard feelings. I want you to get this part. I really do. But you know, other things will come up."

I am a professional. Normally, I would never let a bad mood prevent me from giving a focussed performance. I always know how to kill the tangent thoughts that creep in when I'm trying to inhabit the character's body and vice versa. But Pinchable Cheeks had opened an abyss of thought that swallowed me, and I grew deaf to the lines I was reciting to him, disappearing into his smoulder and further into my insecurities, and finally, after having turned a few dark corners around a cliff, into my worst fear: obsolescence. A theory of mine was starting to come true, a mathematical equation almost as crazy as the Pi theorem, and it would explain the entirety of my life as plainly as a chain of DNA laid out for examination.

There, standing in front of my nemesis that afternoon, I realized that he was easing me into death, the death of who I had become. I was starting the first year of a five-year prison sentence, a period of exile and limbo. It had to do with age and numbers. At forty, I was too old to be hip, but too young to be distinguished. To be an actor between the ages of forty and forty-four in the film industry is to be a corpse walking through a cemetery, grasping at whatever script pages you can clutch in your zombie hands. Being temporarily dead, unable to land any good roles, everything you do is an embarrassment and a scab on your achievements: people run away from you so you can't be photographed together, so your stink won't cling to them and affect their job prospects; they don't return your phone calls or answer your emails, don't talk to you at lunch even though you have adjoining tables, separated only by fear and question marks on their part and disappointment and resignation on yours. You are the condemned and the hopeless. And if, only if you manage to endure the five years, to wander through it intact without damaging yourself too much and without having dragged down your peers and devalued their stock, and if you can somehow prove that you grew throughout the horrible experience, that you learned something, only then will people start to talk to you again. I don't care about the exceptions, the people who fight the onset of age, desperate to be on either side of the five-year desert, anything but caught in the middle and left to die, fudging their birth dates on IMDb, launching plastic surgery campaigns, having intergenerational flings with seniors to make themselves feel young, or buying designer canes from a West Hollywood medical supplies boutique to appear older, decrepit, and perfectly hireable. I don't care about these people because my theory, like all mathematical theories, must be impermeable to exceptions.

Yes, I got all of this just from staring into the eyes of someone I wanted to see dead.

Pinchable Cheeks snapped me back to the casting call by repeating his last few lines. But they made no sense to me, because I had already begun my prison sentence. I had lost my place in the script and didn't know how to respond. It was all just text highlighted in green. I could wing it, but chances are I would say something mean and inappropriate.

A few weeks later, I found out that Pinchable Cheeks got the part.

That was both the confirmation and the undoing of my theory. For as true as it started to seem, I wanted to break it, punch holes in the logic. It was the only way I was going to survive. At the time, I didn't know how to prepare for exile. So I convinced myself that mathematicians were a crazy and deluded group of people whose interpretations were creative, not scientific, who based assumptions on other assumptions, and then, if the ridiculousness cancelled itself out, accepted that as a resolution. Fucking psychotic. And I was an actor. I had no business messing with numbers. I convinced myself that I was still young enough to get the jobs I wanted and old enough to assuage investors that I was a solid bet. I would always be charming. Forty was going to be a great year.

But I was going to have to take opportunities wherever I could find them, even under circumstances that were troublingly unclear.

2.

I KNEW CHRIS CULPEPPER was a crazy bat the minute I met him. We were at a post-premiere party for the film of a mutual friend. Chris was chugging a glass of wine in the corner, sitting with a woman who I assumed was his girlfriend. A little younger than him, and looking bored. Her hair was the kind of bob that took either an hour or five minutes to sculpt. Impossible to tell.

A bratty pianist in a tux was playing Dmitri Shostakovich's seventh symphony on the black baby grand. My second most favourite piece of music. A never-ending plane crash of atonal ideas so sharp and wonderful. Shostakovich composed it in Leningrad while the city was under siege. Genius flourished under threat of death. Musicians showed up to practice worn, hungry, demoralized, and afraid. They tested out new movements while no doubt dreaming of thick chunky stews and a lifespan that extended past the following week. The music kept their minds from shattering altogether.

The director of the film received a rousing toast, and that's when Chris got up from his chair. Woozy and sloshing, an exaggerated drunk. They had apparently known each other in college. With no slurring whatsoever, surprising given his state, Chris began to recite movie lines as performed by Peter Sellers in *The Party*, in which he plays bumbling Indian actor Hrundi V. Bakshi. It wasn't funny. The accent was atrocious. The director made excuses on Chris's behalf to the horrified party guests, but they cleared the room nonetheless. Chris's girlfriend sat in the corner and said nothing, didn't intervene in the car crash in progress. Peter Sellers was fresh in my heart. I had spent the week steeped in Heavenly Hash ice cream and TV marathons of his films. The Kubricks hit me hard. You have to be a genius to splinter so effortlessly into the numerous characters in Dr. *Strangelove*. That's why I loved Chris's impromptu performance, jackass or not. It was the ultimate tribute to Sellers. I knew on the spot I wanted to work with him. I would introduce myself only once he broke character, because it would be too intimidating to interact with even a facsimile of Peter Sellers. Peter, or Chris, caromed into another room in search of fans and drink.

His girlfriend got up calmly and walked over to me. She was wearing a bias-cut dress, all crazy triangles like the Guggenheim.

"Hi, Michael-David, I'm Diane."

"Hi, Diane."

I shook her hand and then realized she hadn't offered it. I grabbed limp fingers that only came to life halfway during the shake. It was a weird exchange.

"Never mind him," she said.

"Actually, I kind of like it."

"I get it. It's hilarious. But forgive me, it's just hard to watch someone self-destruct. It's impossible to love someone who doesn't love themselves. Fuck-face. Not you. Him."

A young man in a tuxedo came by to fill our glasses with Pinot. I didn't know what to make of her.

"Sorry," she continued. "I shouldn't be dumping on you like this. And I shouldn't be bashing Chris. He wants to work with you. But don't tell him I told you."

"He said that? Tell me more."

"Oh, I really shouldn't have said anything. You actors are always so worried about that stuff. Who wants to play with who and why. It's like a kindergarten. Big crybabies. Big, rich crybabies. Worse than the people I work with."

"What do you do?"

"State health administrator. Which means I research what funding goes into anti-smoking campaigns, especially the ones that don't work. The failures when we pump millions into printing badly designed posters of lung cancer. But they usually get the off-setting wrong, so you can't see the cancer. It's just fuzzy blobs. Abstract art. Of course, people are going to keep smoking. Then I pull the plug on the money. I like to think it's so we can put the money to better use, but ..."

"I've always thought it was ridiculous how people are trying to get Garfunkel to give up cigarettes, so he could go on a reunion tour."

"But he hates Paul Simon."

"Everybody hates Paul Simon."

We smiled at each other.

"Listen," she said. "I don't want you to think I'm always depressed like this."

"There's nothing wrong with that. It's your right to be sad."

What a fuckup. I had just reduced someone's depression to mere sadness, a bad mood. There are chemical components involved in depression; it's a complex animal. So I was surprised when Diane suddenly wrapped her arms around me and gave me a hug. I was shocked, actually. She did it in such a familiar way, as if I were an old friend whose body she knew. In this embrace, with my chin perched on the shoulder of her weird dress, I thought about her boyfriend, the man supposedly about to offer me a job.

"How exactly is he self-destructing?"

"It was great to meet you."

"Can't you tell me?"

"I'm sure you can imagine it. Isn't that what actors do? Imagine all the little details of someone's life so you can figure out why they act a certain way? Don't tell me you get all that money for nothing."

She winked and walked away.

"Diane?"

I watched her for a while, sipping her wine into quiet oblivion. She pretended not to notice me. It was that obvious.

I eventually noticed that Chris had come back into the room. He was hovering over the catering table, an ethical fishing nightmare: bluefin tuna finger sandwiches, Russian caviar, breaded starfish, deep-fried sea anemone bloomers, and a sickening centrepiece of a shark on ice, its tail peeled back to reveal the meat. I felt pukey going near the table, but I had to find out what this evening was all about.

"You nailed it," I said, stifling a wretch.

"Not really. Bakshi was more apologetic."

"True, but you were playing Sellers as Bakshi. It gets more complex the more layers you add."

"Tell me."

Chris now appeared clear-eyed and sober. His drunkenness could've been an act, too. He looked kind of horny.

"Well, there's also you," I continued. "The actor can't remove himself from the equation. That's why method acting is kind of a sham."

"Ha. Exactly. What are you doing for work these days?"

"Research."

I wasn't about to reveal my situation to him, even though he probably knew and was just playing dumb. Word travels fast in this town. Chris smeared a Stoned Wheat Thin with an unidentifiable paste. His smile leaned insidiously in my direction.

"Let's take a break from this place and go for a drive. There's something I've been meaning to talk to you about."

"Are you okay to drive?" I asked.

He didn't answer.

Chris took me up to Mulholland Drive. Because of the twists, we saw stretches of road only a hundred feet at a time, when we rounded a bend and the headlights had pavement to hit. Pavement rich with the blood of James Dean, assuming that L.A. is a single, long road, which it kind of is. After a while, he parked the car on the shoulder where we had a clear view of glowing L.A. We were edged on the promontory in front of the scraggly shrubs that tumbled down Runyon Canyon into blackness. There were probably a few lost cars down there, skeletons still buckled up. Suicides, for sure.

I couldn't stop thinking about the Bible, one of the greatest screenplays ever. There's a scene where the Devil takes Jesus to a mountain overlooking the world and offers him glory, riches, debauchery. The part called for dizziness. "This showcase can be yours if you perform an act of worship to me." I wondered if there was some sacrifice I could make, some way to appease the darkness so I could get back into its good graces. So, when Chris offered me a part in his new film, I almost blurted out a yes on the spot. I used to be more of an old-fashioned type who believed in not putting out on the first date, but I had since lost a few of the usual proprieties. However, I had enough self-control to tell him I'd let him know in a few weeks.

The film: an abused boy frees a pack of wolves that his dad has raised, and he runs away with them into the woods. Life in the wilderness teaches him survival, loyalty, and love. He eventually makes his way to the city a man full of kindness, and with a posse of kickass pets. Maybe they terrorize Los Angeles in some kind of dogpocalypse? It was hard to read Chris because he was being vague. The point is that the boy assumes a new identity. This is how people remake themselves, and it's never how you think it'll turn out. Chris said he didn't know how to start a script for this, but he could visualize it. Hunger from page to page, fear and the hard grit. The beautiful uncertainty of losing plot threads. The story has to fall apart for it to be great. Anyways, that's what he told me. People become suspicious when things make too much sense. Only liars have perfect stories because they spend all their time trying not to be discovered. They spin, weave, bob until it's seamless. The problem is that you can't get in, because there are no holes in the lining. The audience isn't part of the film.

Back home, over the next few weeks, I watched all of Chris's films in chronological order, hoping to grasp the evolution of his style and how I fit in. I went through the behind-the-scenes footage numerous times. You can tell a lot about a director's working methods from his body language. Look at his stance on the set. Does it reveal fairness? Are his expectations flexible or is he a tyrant? Will he flip out if an actor goes off-script while the cameras are rolling? I tried to figure this out while watching him interact with the talent, the crew. I observed his fingers operate expensive machinery. There are lessons in the micro-movements. A sure hand with no twitching might indicate a sense of entitlement, and that could be bad news.

Ultimately, I learned very little about Chris through his films, because he seemed to scrub himself out of the work. A sense of erasure seemed to bloom year by year. Maybe it was an allergy to style that heightened with each new project. This curiously measured lack of consistency turned me on. He appeared to use every scene to test out new techniques. The first half of his 1997 black comedy Drill Bits uses jump cuts to expose the ironies of a roommate situation involving a construction worker and a design student. They remodel the place and simultaneously demolish it in order to gain distance from each other. The breakfast counter is both communal space and border patrol, a front and frontier for mutual attraction. Halfway into the film, Chris discards irony for romance and sentimentalism. The camera lingers on moist eyes, forkfuls of shared food. In other films of his, the lack of resolution is epic, threads left dangling as the credits rolled. The lighting was never the same from film to film. This was all reassuring to me in terms of working with him. I would not be locked into a predefined box. There was room to run on the set, and he would have to trust me. One doubt remained. Could the lack of style be an extreme style? Maybe only a dictator had the energy, will, and mania required to avoid repeating himself.

I took a quick walk down Franklin Boulevard, and that was enough to dispel that line of thinking as pre-commitment jitters on my part. Our collaboration was going to be great. He wanted me to play RR, the wolf boy as an adult after he comes to the city with all the wisdom of the wild. This was how Chris had pitched it to me that night on Mulholland Drive. I instantly recognized it as a character that could not only rescue my career, but also grow me as a person.

I called Chris.

"Hi, it's me."

"Hi, you. What have you been up to?"

It was uncouth to tell someone you've been wallowing in their past, judging their documented history of mistakes and perfections. It could be embarrassing.

"Reading scripts," I lied. "Speaking of which, when are you going to send me one?"

"Is that a yes?"

"I really like the concept, and I like the part. It's ..." I looked around my living room for an answer, as if expecting to find it in the Persian hand-woven rugs and the avant-garde artwork. Things in an apartment I'm now trying hard to forget. "It's redeeming."

"Exactly. Living as a wolf teaches him priorities that he can then apply to any life circumstance."

"I also like how he doesn't take revenge."

"Right," Chris said.

"What's it called?"

"I have a few titles bouncing around."

"Bounce one over to me."

"They're just preliminary."

"When can I read the script?"

"Well, I'm writing it as we speak, and I'll probably still be writing while we shoot. Your part is contingent on what happens with the boy. Child actors these days can really fuck things up. But I'm glad you're on board. Your agent would never let you say yes without a script. This is about trust between you and me."

"Who says I said yes?"

"You don't have to say anything."

"Tell me more about RR."

"You want to know what he's like? Cruelly intelligent, but he doesn't let anyone know it. He analyzes everything sideways and inside out but it doesn't disrupt his outer calm. RR is a master survivalist, but too weak to hunt. His flaw is that he prefers to stay put and defend against attackers rather than go kill them where they sleep."

"Are we talking literally or figuratively?"

"A bit of both. There are some lessons he should learn in the wild but doesn't."

"He sounds a bit like me," I joked.

"RR is a bit like everybody."

"Can you at least send a synopsis to me?

"Sure, but it'll be a rough draft. You know how these things go."

I sucked at negotiating. After I hung up, it struck me I might have difficulty trusting someone who can eat so close to a murdered shark.

True to his word, Chris sent the synopsis to me. I showed it to my agent, Sandy. We analyzed it over beef carpaccio. We were still embarrassed about the outcome of the last audition, and we were probably both to blame, but our mutual love of food was great enough to put that nightmare aside temporarily.

It was a loose kind of writing. Sentences trailed off into ellipses and thoughts that could go either way. Cliff-hangers disappeared into the void between paragraphs. The characters were oblique, and RR was the least developed of all of them. There was no description about how he looked or dressed. Squat on mannerisms or ways of speech. We tried to track the parallel plot lines by drawing them on napkins, confused that our lines of blue and green ink never criss-crossed.

The boy lives with his dad on a farm. The dad raises wolves for a living. He's a violent, short-tempered man, but he refuses to subject his prize wolves to the ugliness. Instead, he turns on the boy. Pitchfork upside the head. Lashed with a garden hose. Put to work twelve hours a day, working in the fields to the point of exhaustion. There is no mom character. Outwardly, the dad wants to grow his boy hard and resilient. The truth is that he needs a human punching bag, or he'll end up beating a costly wolf to death. The only respite for the boy is his trombone. He dreams all day of playing it. When nettles prick his delicate skin, a hologram of the trombone forms in his mind, braying loud and sliding at full tilt. F, D, B♭, D, F, B♭. The boy begins to see the furrows in the field as sheet music, and plants seeds accordingly, notes on a staff. He comes in from the field bruised and caked with manure. Of course, he's too late for dinner. He showers away the shame, retreats to his bedroom, and plays the trombone. He stuffs it with socks to mute the noise and not piss off his dad. The vibrations make him happy.

But the boy can't live this way anymore. He frees the wolves from their cages and escapes with them into the wilderness. It's a struggle to survive. The wolves bring him dead mangled squirrels and ptarmigans full of nourishing organs to eat. The boy learns to suppress his gag reflex. Rawness. Frostbitten pink genitals. A runny nose full of icicles. It is here where the boy becomes RR, a new identity free of his past and its pain. It's a name he gives himself, because before that, he was always called "boy." RR snuggles with the wolf pack in the snow. He knows that a wolf could forget its manners and devour him at any moment. But that doesn't happen. He releases his childhood anguish into the hard work of survival and grows to become a kind young man. RR continues to practice his trombone in the woods, scaring away game and frustrating the wolves. When parts break off due to normal wilderness wear-and-tear, he sticks them back together with pine tar. He soon grows a beard but has nothing to shave it with. The wolves howl in approval. This RR will never use razors, they chortle.

Meanwhile, with no boy and no wolves, the dad turns his rage on the dogs, breeding pups just so he can chop off their ears.

At one point, Sandy's and my pen lines came within a quarter inch of each other, and I got excited. We ordered cappuccino and biscotti to celebrate the breakthrough, but the criss-cross never happened. The story fizzled to the edge of the napkin and beyond. I just sat there and sogged my rock-hard cookie in coffee to make it edible.

"This is a good sign," Sandy said.

"What are you talking about? It doesn't tie together. When RR goes to the city and joins the symphony, his father doesn't even come to see him perform."

"I thought you said you were happy there was no revenge."

"That's not revenge, that's resolution. And this movie has none. You're supposed to steer me away from crazy ideas."

"You're calling it a 'movie'? How base. Anyways, it's better than an ending that's too clean."

"Fine. But where's he going with this? Can you tell?"

"Michael-David, you need to take risks. Sometimes the most beautiful work comes from chaos like this. Chris has a reputation for being this way. The point is, do you trust him?"

"I don't know."

"Well, you have to figure that out."

There were a few obstacles to trust. It had nothing to do with sharks. Maybe it was my paranoia acting up, but I grew suspicious of the project. It sounded like a made-up vehicle Chris was using to get close to me for some reason. How come I hadn't already heard of it? Studio gossip rarely bypasses me. And there was no script and no other attached actors he could name. Zilch on IMDb.

But I didn't want to let fear rule my life, so I gave Chris the benefit of the doubt. I fantasized about escaping into RR, into his skin and life and out of my own despair. He seemed to have an inner light that had been extinguished in me. The perfect host. To make it happen, I'd have to play him believably enough to fool myself.

I signed on the invisible dotted line.

It turned out to be a real production, and I was ecstatic to find my fears were misplaced. Bodies hustled across the lot, sweaty under the weight of props, electric cables, and thermoses of gourmet coffee. Arguments over power supplies and voltage. Sinuous chatter about rejected permits to film in the city and who they should call for help. This is the kind of environment that energized me. This was my set, but these were not my problems. It was the lull before I opened my mouth and before anything could go wrong. Nobody could fault me in the world between disasters. I was a silent film star for a few precious hours every afternoon, nosing in and out of trouble innocently, leaving the mess for others to clean up. I wandered into the carpentry studio when they were on break and set my coffee cup down on a stack of set design blueprints. It's surreal to stare into plans for a world that someone is designing for you. I looked for a Jacuzzi but couldn't find one. How disappointing. They didn't expect me to sit in the ice between takes, did they? I picked up my coffee and took a sip. The cup left a Jacuzzi-shaped ring on the drawings.

Shooting began with a skeleton crew working on a need-to-know basis, and resources were added as the production grew. Grip, gaffer, best boy, makeup technician. Giant soft box lights like marshmallows suspended in the air. The set designer had to make the plastic look like grass. First, we shot the scenes without dialogue. Chris and the acting coach discouraged me from hamming it up. Through their constant criticisms from the sidelines, they shaped my plastic face to have no expression. "That's the music's job," they reminded me. The days of mooning lids and pouty kissers were gone with the weekend matinee. I played it straight and in stillness, enduring the lights with Billy, who played RR as a boy. We shot anachronistically, bouncing around in time in a film we knew almost nothing about. They wanted Billy and me to be together on the set, so we could bond artistically and I could be a positive older male influence on him.

It was a big day when Chris gave us the first script pages. He had come in after lunch, unshaven and wearing shades. At first Billy and I suspected it was alcohol, but Chris explained he had been up all night writing and editing. The lines were fresh from his brain. The text was writhing with typos. When Billy and I helped each other rehearse on the first run-throughs, we always read the typos as-is for a laugh. At night, when the cast and crew had dinner and wine, Chris would be in his trailer scribbling on yellow legal pads. Without his furious writing, there would be no tomorrow. We learned to leave him alone and not to ask questions. It was more fun that way. Billy and I clicked, and we spent a lot of our time off together. I took him to see a NASCAR race at the Auto Club Speedway. We screamed at the pieces of brightly coloured metal hurtling by on melting rubber, donkeying advertisements around the oval at 200 miles an hour. We ended the day with oversize turkey drumsticks and fries. Of course, I peeled off the skin and patted my fries with tissue to lower my fat intake. I believe that harm reduction techniques should be applied to fast food, if nothing else. I gave Billy a road beer in a paper bag, because I felt he might be expecting it. He guzzled it.

My relations with the rest of the crew and cast were good, too. Charlie was a treat to work with. She gave "suspecting rural postal worker" a new standard, all haggard looks and withering cigarettes. My coffee cup was never empty because I always gave the gofer my best Culpepper-doing-Sellers-doing-Bakshi impressions. The snow guy explained the science behind making ice in summer, and he didn't have to.

The wolf wrangler insisted I meet the dogs.

"Dogs?" I asked. "Aren't wolves a breed of their own?"

"Technically, yes," she said. "But would you call your kids 'humans' or 'kids'? Wait till you meet them. You'll see."

I saw, all right. Rippling waves of muscles under silver-tipped fur. Blue and grey eyes, usually mismatched in a cute kind of way. Those Venetian-white teeth were spotless; the wrangler must've scrubbed the muskrat guts out of them daily. The trainer demoed how to approach them safely, palms upward and below waist level.

"Don't be afraid. They won't bite."

These were my dogs, after all. I figured I had better get to know them for authenticity's sake, if I ever wanted to rescue them, and RR to rescue me. Despite the bristling manes, they were sweethearts. One of them licked my hand incessantly, no doubt crazy for the bacon in the pasta carbonara they had served for lunch. Nights, I retired to my star suite trailer and read up on wolves. The trainer had suggested a number of books on pack psychology, their endangered status, and heart-warming relationships between human and wolf. There was one entry about a wolf owner stranded in a remote Arctic area who lost a finger to frostbite. His dog was starving, so he offered it the finger, but it refused out of loyalty. The man pretended to eat the finger, but the dog wouldn't budge. He had to chew and swallow his own fingernail for the dog to accept the dead, discoloured meat. It swallowed without chewing and stared hungrily at the four live fingers on its owner's hand, which the man had to keep hidden from the dog's view for the rest of the ordeal.

I spent more time with the dogs, usually in the mornings, while waiting for Chris to arrive with new pages of the script. I learned how to pet them and I gained their trust through a kind but firm touch. We started to wrestle. They slammed me to the ground, playfully choking me with the lightest of bites. These animals were clean, more sanitary than most people I know.

Even though I was on excellent terms with the dogs, the trainer never left us alone.

"You just never know," she said.

I think she was jealous of our connection.

3.

MY STAR SUITE WAS THE Cadillac of trailers, the Rolls-Royce of wheeled storage containers. It had a fancy all-in-one kitchenette with ceramic hot and cold faucets, a reclining massage chair, a stocked bar with icemaker, a sound system with subwoofers, a TV I didn't use, and a skylight. The sun's rays cut horizontally through the Plexiglas and reflected off the wall onto me. It was nice to tan in the residual glow of the sunset and keep some colour. The bathroom was more of a cabinet than a room. That was the scariest part. If I locked myself in there accidentally, there was no way to escape. My screams would only echo and deafen me, because trailers are soundproof, and the only ventilation is in the main living area. This was before I grew to like enclosed spaces.

More frightening stuff: the front door had a deadbolt. If there was a fire at night and I forgot to keep the key in the lock, Michael-David would become Michael-David's charred remains. Yes, the spectre of death makes me refer to myself in the third person. There are many reasons I don't smoke, and that's definitely one of them.

Because of these various fear factors, at night I went home to my old life.

I never thought I would hang out with Chris again, at least not until shooting wrapped up. But we did, when he wasn't losing his mind trying to write before scotch eroded his motor skills after full days of trying to keep the production on schedule, viewing and reviewing dailies with dozens of people who gave feedback of varying usefulness, and refereeing squabbles on set. Ego stuff, usually. Diva hissy fits and arguments about seniority. Everybody is uncomfortable under the lights. Sweat is the hidden price of glamour.

I was surprised when Chris knocked on the door of my trailer one evening, before I'd left for home. I had assumed it was the wardrobe guy for a "fitting," which was becoming a tired excuse for feeling up my thighs and chest. But it was Chris. He looked ten years older than when I'd first met him only a few months before.

"Can I take you out for a beer?"

I agreed, though I wondered what was up. Maybe he meant "beer" the same way people suggest you go for "coffee" together. Random beverages always mean bad news.

He drove me in his Sebring to a watering hole on east Santa Monica Boulevard, a dive lit in Heineken green and Budweiser red, Christmas-style neon. Chris ordered a triple Glenlivet. I ordered mineral water.

"I need your advice on the script," he said, before his drink arrived, the first in what turned into a flotilla.

"Why me?"

"Well, you're the only one who's interested in it."

"Sure, but answer me this. How did you get the production going without a script?"

"Ha ha. Has that been driving you crazy? Fuck, man. You need to slide a finger in your asshole and loosen it up. Here's some more unsolvable shit. How did we end up making a movie using wolves without PETA picketing in the studio parking lot every day? How did you manage to even get this role"—Chris paused to lick the salt off a nacho—"when you've never done this kind of work before?"

"What do you mean?" I was miffed, but not sure why.

"Work with animals."

"They're wolves, not animals. And I don't even know what the role is."

"You kill me! What a guy. What I'm saying is that these are the mysteries of working in movies. Things happen. And once they do, they come at you like a wall of water. It's irreversible."

Irreversible. The word stuck in my head. Mainly because my life had felt irreversible from the day I first met Chris. Before him, I had an escape plan for everything.

"What kind of help do you need?" I asked.

"Inspiration for one of the parts. The actor playing it is a supreme asshole."

Supreme Asshole played my abusive father. I hate Supreme Asshole, and I had no idea why Chris cast him, an actor utterly without talent, coasting on an angular jaw and a goofy look. Of *course* he pulled off that role in *Batman*. Put *anyone* in a funky costume and watch it empower them. I avoided him when we crossed paths in wardrobe or on our way to the trailer suites. I think Supreme Asshole could sense my distaste for him.

"Why do you think I can help with that?"

"You have a dad, right?"

My mind instantly scanned every magazine article about me I had come across that referenced my family. I get a paper jam every time I do this mental exercise.

"He wasn't abusive," I said. I had never spoken on the record about my dad. And yet, Chris seemed to know something.

"I'm sure he wasn't. But our dads all miss the mark every other Thursday, know what I mean? They expect too much, or forget something really important. Maybe he was mean to someone you loved, and you never forgot it. I was just hoping you could tell me about your dad. Or anyone's dad. I need some input a.s.a.p. because my script is fucking dying."

So, I talked. My dad was a good provider of material sustenance. As a point of entry I chose the roaming construction jobs he always took, transplanting us across the country. Bridge work in Wyoming. Viaducts in Indianapolis. The sidewalks in Memphis were all cracked to shit, and old ladies tripped into too many lawsuits. He hated to see a job half done, so my dad would go back after midnight to fix the mistakes his co-workers had made. It wasn't unusual for cops in Topeka, Kansas, to find my dad slinking around building scaffolding in the dark, straightening the supports with a sledgehammer and a level. He was a perfectionist. I found this type of character sketching harmless, so I didn't feel vulnerable. I blabbed about his eating and drinking habits, and the type of cigarettes he smoked. I explained how I would make shadow puppets in the blue clouds puffing out of his mouth.

Chris started to drink at a faster clip when I mentioned the cigarettes.

Then I went where I shouldn't have gone. I told him about the toy xylophone I had had as a kid. Multi-coloured metal plates you hit with a plastic drumstick. Ping, ping, pong. One day my father was working on his poo-brown Camaro, a car that always broke down but which we always forgave because it was like a machine replica of Tom Selleck—suave and headstrong, with a moustachioed license plate. I was pinging away in my room when my father walked in, covered in monkey grease. Strangely, he asked to borrow my xylophone. I reluctantly let him have it. He took the xylophone for several hours. I could hear my dad working in the garage directly under my room. I pressed my ear to the floor to listen for musical sounds but heard nothing. I stayed in that position for hours, afraid to venture into the garage, a mechanic's slaughterhouse. Later, he knocked on the door to my room, came in, and handed me a xylophone missing all its teeth except for one, the highest and plinkiest key. I was shattered, and my tears came quickly. I knew this disaster had something to do with the car. For weeks I refused to take a trip anywhere in the Camaro. I even walked to school in the rain. Finally, one day, I had no choice and got in. As the car peeled out of the driveway, engine huffing smoothly (which was out-of-character), I heard a plink in the key of C and melted in the back seat. The engine had stolen my music because my dad had been too cheap to buy replacement parts. Bad luck that my xylophone had been the closest available substitute.

I never got a new one.

The conversation was getting too heavy for me. I had to change the subject.

"Why don't we talk about your father," I said.

"I don't have one. He was just sperm on paper. Technically, I'm a bastard."

Then we went for a game of black light bowling, where we tossed gutterballs beside army brats and prom queens. Chris's teeth and dandruff were ultraviolet white under the rays. We both refused to wear the bowling shoes, Chris because he gets defiant when he's drunk, and me because they are so unfashionable. Chris was all over the place and slipped on the oiled parquet a few times. He's a hefty man, and he fell hard. With five frames left in our game, we surrendered the lane to some kids. Chris tried to persuade me to go to a strip club for a nightcap, but I declined. I was the relatively sober one, so I took charge of preserving our professional relationship. I also doubt we could've chosen a club that both of us would like. I had a feeling he wanted to go to French's Nudes on Santa Monica. I didn't like it that they had no windows.

The next afternoon, a set assistant handed me new scenes to

rehearse. I read them and was confused. Since when did RR have a gun? In all the discussions I'd had with Chris, I never got the impression that RR was the weapon-toting type—the opposite, in fact. He was searching for peace. A gun would undermine RR's retreat into nature to rebuild himself as a person. You cannot escape human cruelty if you carry its tools. A firearm was a flaw in the script, a bug that would corrupt the pages one at a time until the whole thing was unreadable. Even worse, I would lose RR as a role model, and Billy would lose me. I couldn't believe it.

And I'm terrified of guns. I've always known I'll die by getting shot. Don't ask me where this information comes from. But I can feel with my fingers where the bullet holes will be. Six entry wounds in the lower back, five exit wounds in the chest. The shooter will probably be kneeling behind me. I'll be buried with the sixth bullet inside me. It will never be recovered.

And how the hell does RR get a gun in the wilderness?

I went looking for Chris to convince him a rewrite was necessary but I couldn't find him. Props called me in for a fitting. The weapon had to be comfortable in my hand. I couldn't lose grip while running through fake snow swinging my arms. See the trigger as an extension of the hand. Steel fulfills what the bone wishes. The props master was a forty-something perpetual frat boy wearing a promotional Lakers T-shirt, the cheapie kind they cannonade into the stands during commercial breaks. He smiled as he slipped the weapon into my hand and closed my fingers around the cold metal, no doubt imagining the gore he'd get to make because of my character's proclivities for violence. The gun was modelled on a Harrington & Richardson .32 calibre revolver, he told me. It was my first time holding a gun, but it didn't feel fake. The heaviness in my hand filled me with rage. I wanted to shoot the props master in the face, and then turn his ugly shirt into Swiss cheese. This was not my path in cinema. I felt queasy, and looked around for containers that would hold vomit. A Mad Hatter's bowler would do fine. I pictured strands of Johnny Depp's hair floating in my regurgitated oatmeal sludge.

I thought about the adage that says, when you introduce a gun, it has to go off by the third act. I wasn't a killer, and neither was RR. Even if I never fired a shot in the film, this weapon would bring out all of my bad qualities, give me a taste for revenge. After I shot up the props master, Chris would get six bullets in the chest. You could consider them lead merit badges for dishonesty. The wolves and I would trot down Sunset Boulevard and pick off the editors-in-chief guilty of spreading lies about me and then feast on their limbs. How would that stalker kid feel with the cold barrel chipping his teeth and pressing against his tonsils? Oh, I haven't told you about him yet.

I'd had enough.

"Um, you can't leave with that. You can't carry a gun on set if you're not shooting."

I looked at him point blank.

"I mean if they're not shooting," he corrected himself nervously.

"Sorry."

I didn't realize I was still holding it.

"No worries. We need to find you a .22. You don't look comfortable holding the .32. I'll bring it out to you."

Over the next few weeks, as I reluctantly carried the gun around set with me, it strangely began to feel natural. And I felt the mood around me shift. There was a palpable darkness, a sense of quiet that wasn't calming. The normally friendly crew stopped joking with me. They started to be more formal. It was shocking when the gofer asked me what I "required" in my coffee, instead of what I "wanted." Besides, he should've known by then that I took it black. The crew grabbed food from the catering table and ate it in their private quarters, instead of out in the open where I could join them. When the makeup woman squinted, was she responding to the excessive light or trying to reduce eye contact with me? Even Billy didn't seem himself around me. I wondered what I had done to alienate him. Strained relations with youth sting me with a particular guilt. I can't handle the responsibility of closing a heart so young. That's probably why I never had kids—they all grow up to hate and hurt you. I asked Billy out to NASCAR again, but he said he was busy, even though I knew he had nothing to do but play video games in his trailer. So, I sat alone in my trailer reading and responding to Facebook and Twitter fan messages with a fading sense of optimism. The last sunny tweets went out as the clouds closed in over me.

I shot the remainder of my scenes in those last weeks. RR had to kill his own food, which meant pointing my gun at stuffed animals perched in plastic trees. A wrangler hustled stunt grouse in and out of cat carriers. I got birdseed under my fingernails. This was the unmagical part of Hollywood, when you go so far into the nuts and bolts of illusion that you wonder how it can ever look real. The biggest disappointment for me was to learn that when RR went to the city, he was armed. Strange how a farm boy had never heard the Johnny Cash song "Don't Take Your Guns to Town." Another bug in the script. His years in the wilderness hadn't redeemed him, from what I could tell. All that time alone had made him bitter. From a position of safety behind the lights, Chris grew abrupt and terse in giving me instructions, and it brought out the natural creases in my face. Frown lines pushed out, the height of their topographical ridges in proportion to my mounting unhappiness. In the end, he got what he wanted: an angry face. It bothered me that there was now a security guard on set. Could the gun be real?

The damage grew day by day. We were doing more than just making a bad movie that caved in to public hunger for violence and revenge. We were destroying me. I had already made a significant effort becoming RR in hopes of saving myself. I recreated his personality in my heart, his life in my head. RR's memories soon took their place beside mine, supplanted them. Images of ploughs, hay bales, and cracked hands sank into my own childhood. Sneaking mouthfuls of fresh chewing tobacco behind the shed. Washing the bell of a trombone with lake water and then polishing it in the sun. Instant shine. I immersed myself in a love of wolves. I believed there was hope for escaping horrible situations. You could reinvent your life by taking drastic action. But now RR was becoming a fiend. I suspected he would kill someone before the movie was over. Maybe my screen dad, Supreme Asshole. A lone bullet would kill him, but it would really be killing me. There was no way to back out of this disaster contractually. I would have to pursue it to the end, let it consume what was left of my joy and optimism. I could disavow the character, but it would live on in the movies. I would always be the angry guy on the poster. The killer lives on in myth like no other.

I needed to talk to Chris about this, but he was avoiding me. He always split as soon as a scene was done, and he didn't answer my calls. I wouldn't have been so unprofessional as to talk with him during shooting, so I held back, glaring at him instead. I had so much to say to him, and it built up inside me like sewage, layer after toxic layer. I saw an opportunity to vent one day when Charlie had to be sent back to hair and makeup, and it created a delay on set. Chris had no orders to bark, no technical glitches to obsess over, no new lines to write. Nowhere to run from me. So I stalked over from the soundstage and saw the apprehension on his face.

"Hey," I said.

"Hi."

"You never said anything about a gun."

"Oh, that? I didn't even know about it until recently."

"Don't play innocent, it makes you look stupid."

Chris looked away for a second and watched a stage hand restuffing an industrial garbage bag with Styrofoam snow granules. She didn't know there was a hole in the bag. Fake ice pissed on her shoes. The bag was never going to fill up.

"Please be reasonable," he finally said to me.

"The gun has been making me want to shoot everyone in the face. Doesn't matter who. It's like a bad mood that grows and grows, and it's not me at all. I'm not doing another fucking scene with this thing, period."

We both looked at my empty hand. I was talking like I was still holding the weapon. I felt silly, a whiny child. But I wasn't the one who had to answer for his actions—Chris was. I had the feeling that if I was holding the gun, and if it were real, shit would happen. I would force the tip of the barrel into his nostril, fire a bullet into his last thought and scatter it like lightning. But not before shooting a new booze hole in his throat.

"Listen, things have been changing. I've been meaning to talk to you."

"Oh, really. When?"

"It's too early to understand what's going on. Michael-David, I need you to trust me. That's how we work around here."

I was on the verge of reciting a point-form list of the ways in which he'd lost my trust when a microphone went dead and he was called away to monitor tests on a replacement.

"Sorry," Chris said, and walked away.

We shot the final scene the next day. Billy and Supreme Asshole watched from the sidelines, in a blossoming friendship that irritated me and that I didn't condone. Supreme Asshole was both a poor performer and a poor role model.

It was a busy day on set. We were recreating the pomp and glut of a full orchestra. The crew had built a symphony hall in one of the lots, including stage, seating, and slanted acoustic ceiling with baffles for soundproofing. That week I had asked if I needed to learn the trombone. At least the basic notes. The hell if I was going to let a personal meltdown interrupt any professional research. I might as well win a Razzie for my most deplorable work. But the acting coach told me I wouldn't be playing any notes per se, and the trombone music would be overdubbed and synchronized to footage of me working the slide at different speeds and lengths. At least there was no gun in this scene. That would kill me.

I was the only fake musician. They had bussed in the Sacramento Symphony Orchestra for the day. At the catering tables, they were a hungry bunch, particularly the bassoonists, and they were meticulous about brushing their teeth so that food particles wouldn't get between their blowpipes and sonic perfection. Airholes, I mean. It was quite the sight to witness eight French horn players spitting toothpaste into the bathroom sink in unison.

By then, I had reached a grumpy low, snarling my greetings to each new member of the noise brigade as they disturbed me merely by taking their places in orchestra formation. The acting coach whis-

pered to a distraught cellist that I was in character, and that I had
nothing against the strings. I drained the spit valve of my trombone,
which earned me dirty looks. The brass instrument was polished and
shiny, with an oiled slide that disappeared into the shaft with cool
precision. It was heavier than I expected. I thought back to RR as a boy.
How could a twelve-year-old hold this steady? Perhaps I could find
some serenity in the music, even when I was imprisoned like this.
While I sat in the orchestra in my ridiculously uncomfortable tuxedo,
an assistant delivered a piece of paper to me. It was yellow legal, with
blue handwriting in a decidedly frantic jaunt. Chris's instructions on
physical blocking. Here are the notes I could make out:

> Turn away from camera, it will follow. Only slightly
> though. Give it time to track.

> Take the hexagonal key and undo slide. Bracket at the top
> with screw. You'll see it. Ask Sam if location unclear.

> Dismantle bracing strut with same key. Unlatch the water
> key (spit valve). Don't lose the pieces. This is like IKEA,
> ha ha.

> Turn the counterweight clockwise on the tuning slide,
> unhook the little thingy on the back, it looks like the
> eyelet behind a picture frame.

> Give the pieces to Sam and take a break.

> Shooting again.

Look around twenty times. Thereabouts of course. You don't want to get caught. We'll use the best take, just be consistent.

Counterweight now has blu-tack. Push bracing strut onto it, counterweight below. Then water key. Press everything to tighten. When done, give it to Sam. The props guy will visit you with stuff.

Don't practice this before shooting. Might fuck up trombone and we don't have anyone who knows about reassembly. Michael-David, sorry not much time to talk, we'll do it soon. Thanks.

The orchestra tuned up, and I re-read the notes masquerading as sheet music on the stand in front of me. There would be close-ups of my hands. I chastised myself for not taking better care of them over the years. The knuckle hair was embarrassing. Didn't they keep a fucking aesthetician on staff? Flute. Double bass. Sax. Violin. It relaxed me somewhat. Until then, I had never realized how loud an orchestra actually was. Chris showed up and slinked behind the cameras where we couldn't make eye contact. The director of photography aligned us in Panavision and the lights grew hot. Not only was my collar half an inch too small, but the cotton was blended with synthetics in a thread count too despicably low to mention. So I sat, fumed, and chafed.

Shooting began. The orchestra started playing Shostakovich's seventh symphony. Sublime. Chris must've done it on purpose. It swept me away to Leningrad, 1942. Bombs dropped yet work on the symphony continued. Out of darkness emerged beauty that has lasted for decades and helped others through their heartache, including mine.

I used to play this piece at full volume in my apartment when I was feeling down. Shostakovich did not provide answers or even comfort. It was stability. So that day, shooting the last scene of the movie, I knew things were going to be all right. The music could save me. It was a relief to feel my mood lighten.

Yes, it was a privilege to be associated with this dissonant masterpiece, but it was weird that Culpepper chose it.

The cameras zoomed in. I followed the instructions, glancing surreptitiously at Chris's notes when I forgot what to unscrew. Tiny brass parts rained into my lap. I handed them off to the assistant, and assembled what she handed back. It was like watch-making. But that thought was washed away by a sudden wave of nausea, the crest of a fever. The second movement swelled and circled around me. I felt I was going to be motion sick. For some reason, this section was all xylophone. That's not how it was in the original composition. I could've been eight fucking years old again, crying. I was disassembling the trombone like my dad had taken apart my xylophone all those years ago, bar by bar, note by note. Unbelievable. Chris had used my personal information against me. And now I looked in my hands and saw what I was building. A makeshift gun. I puked a bit into my mouth and swallowed.

Chris walked up to me and whispered into my ear while the music dipped into a minefield of staccato violin notes.

"You have to shoot your dad. He's sitting in the back row."

I strained and saw Supreme Asshole.

Believe it or not, killing him wasn't even fun.

4.

SHOOTING WRAPPED UP. I cleaned out my trailer and went home. What a disaster. When things get bad, I console myself with sex. Like how you might buy yourself a tub of ice cream and bag of chips after a shitty day at work.

This time it was a young man with the avatar "str8sk8rdude." I know, but hey. I'm powerless to this kind of coding. My own avatar was far less creative and not worth mentioning. My pic, a hooded shadow. I included almost no information in my profile, except for will-not-cross boundaries of Olympic Boulevard and the 110 freeway. A chat box popped up on my screen, and str8sk8rdude entered my life as a series of ones and zeros. His profile pic showed him sitting on a skateboard, jeans unzipped and underwear showing. Nothing too racy. He had a buzz cut and a crooked smile. Cute in a Midwestern kind of way.

I believe the madness first sprang as a flirtation, a wink returned with a wink, but with a slightly different mouth. How innocent these emoticons seemed to me back then. They revealed tone, but not genuine emotion, so they did not transgress into the personal and I felt safe. But str8sk8rdude gradually pushed into my world nonetheless.

"what r u up 2?"

"Looking at your sexy pic."

"lets switch 2 cam."

"I don't do that."

I've always hated how reactive I sound in written communications, but I have many reasons to fear being the first to speak.

"then what do u want 2 do?"

"We can just talk."

"how old r u"

"Late thirties."

"like old late thirties?"

"Yes."

"im 19. i guess u can tell from the pic"

"Not really. If ... "

"yeah im 19"

"I believe you, but please give me time to craft my answers before you reply again. I'm not as fast ..."

"Sorry"

"... as you. I really dislike chatting, but I realize that's how things are (r, ha ha) done these days. I was going to say that when I see a skateboard, I assume the guy is at least in his twenties and reliving some kind of nostalgia. Don't guys your age have rollerblades or something?"

" ... "

"Hello?"

"whats nostaljia"

"Fondness for the past."

"okay. but I still have a sk8board"

"I know."

"and im str8"

"Yes, aren't we all."

"do you think I'm sexy?"

"Would it please a young straight man for an older man to find him sexy?"

"what does that even mean"

"What you just asked me."

"oh. you're confusing. but funny. im going to kill myself"
"..."

That was the first time in years that I gave my phone number to a stranger online. Jared called me almost immediately. His voice was raspy with smoke but also a little shaky. He had just run away from home and was staying with a friend in Los Feliz. We talked for about two hours. I didn't say any of the expected things like "don't do it," or "life is worth living," or "it's going to get better, just wait and see." That's not my style. I shut up and listened, prodding Jared for more information with the occasional question. It wasn't charity work. Nothing rips a bigger hole in my heart than a young man in trouble. It was like I kept him on the line to plug the gash and stop the blood flow. Nothing altruistic about it.

Jared was from Pasadena. He'd had to care for his sick parents. Both were dying of cancer, lying in side-by-side deathbeds. Pancreatic, bladder. Nasty stuff, but I never found out who had what. His parents held hands listening to the final murmurs in their bodies. Jared was their adopted son, and when they fell ill without adequate insurance coverage, they turned to him for caretaking. From shit-bored teenager to nurse in a matter of months. Overloaded with responsibility, he had to remortgage the house to pay for their treatments. Jared had to drive each of them to chemo twice a week in a car that the bank would soon repossess. There wasn't even time to smoke up with his friends or play Sony PlayStation. No time to fuck the handsome suburban businessmen in their sexmobiles, not even quick discreet sucks below the steering wheel. It wore him down.

Jared hated his parents' hands most of all. He dreamed of cutting them off, those frail anemic fingers that held each other over the approaching abyss. Their fingers represented evil, he explained to me

49

over the phone. One of his parents had molested him as a kid. Jared didn't specify which, because they were both guilty to him. One guarded the silence of the other. I started to cry. I wanted to hold him and squeeze the pain out.

"Why didn't you say something?"

"They were dying."

"Are they dead now?"

"I don't know."

I wanted to tell him to smother his parents rather than commit suicide. Killing himself would make the injustice all the more mind-numbing, impossible, insane. I couldn't believe the flow of this sex hookup. I thought of something else to say.

"Don't you owe it to yourself to confront them at least once?"

Cringe. A platitude. I hoped this wasn't the end of Jared. I wanted nothing more than to meet in person and crush him with a bear hug, with my lonely gay male love that has found little outlet over the decades.

"I did," he said. "I confronted them."

"And?"

I heard a bubbly sip on the other end of the line, and the clink of ice.

"They said to let sleeping dogs lie. God would judge them in heaven for whatever they did or didn't do, and there was no sense in stirring up trouble on earth when there was so little time left. Dude, they just wanted peace."

The fucker had me bawling. He made no sense in text, had no dimension, but on the phone his voice dismantled me one word at a time until I was gibberish. A quick and troublesome descent. I couldn't take it anymore. I needed to cry in privacy.

"I have to get off the line. Promise me you won't kill yourself."

"Dude, I won't. It has to get a little worse first. But wow. It feels like you're the only one who understands me. Everyone else thinks I'm being a little shit. They have no idea."

I suggested we meet, and he accepted. A flagrant anonymity breach. I knew the implications and was unsure if Jared could handle them. But he seemed different. I felt a special bond growing between us. Maybe only a few filaments, but as windproof as a web. It felt good. I needed emotional release more than a cause, but with Jared it seemed I could get both with no commitment. Name one sane human being who would turn that down.

We met on a restaurant terrace. I expected him to be composed yet falling apart, charmingly incoherent. Carrying himself with equal measures of depression and hope. The kind of person you wanted to help because you saw all of their extremes and, in a flash of happiness, envisioned yourself as the bridge.

Unfortunately, Jared was none of that. The first red flag was that he was almost as well dressed as I was. Kid *sans* skateboard, another bad sign. He asked me to autograph a napkin. I did it out of habit, and asked him how he knew. He said he recognized my voice on the phone but didn't say anything. He admitted that the molesting was fake but the rest was true.

People of the jury, I am a class act. I don't run screaming out of cafés. This bitch holds his ground and, even more importantly, stays rooted in humanity. I'd give the benefit of the doubt to almost anybody. That's just how I am. Everybody deserves an escape hatch, especially confused teens who start life off with the suburbs as a handicap.

"Are you sure it was fake?"

Jared ordered a Long Island Iced Tea. The waiter didn't ask him for I.D.

"Ya. Dunno why I said it. You seemed so nice. My dad still has cancer."

"Pancreas?"

"I think. Not sure. Where is that again?"

I didn't answer.

"Hey, you shouldn't be upset with me," he said. "I'm still depressed."

"Do you lie to every trick you pick up?"

"I thought you cared about me!"

"That wasn't you. This is you."

"I could totally fuck you up, you know. I saved all of our chats. Let's see each other for a while. You really understand me. Don't you know what it means for me to say that?"

There you have it. The hard evidence that I have the worst job in the world. Funny how it's easier to care about someone you don't know. And by funny, I mean unbelievably and unspeakably sad.

"This conversation is over."

I paid the bill, left, and went home to West Hollywood. A totally insecure location. This was the pre-9/11 of my life. I turned the key, thinking it was the end of the embarrassment, that I could regain my scraps of lost privacy. What a fool. I finished reading a novel in my antique New Zealand mahogany bed with a package of dill pickle rice chips and slept soundly until morning.

This is what I saw scrawled on the full length of my door in perma-nent black marker when I opened it and checked the mailbox:

"i hate you because you are the only person who can help me i hate you because you suck i hate you because you are heartless like every other celebrity i hate you because you have no faith in people i hate you because i have a crush on you i hate you because you are sexy i hate you because every time i watch one of your movies i imagine you raping me at gunpoint i hate you because you are you i hate the way you smile it is so fake i hate you because you think all young people are stupid i hate you motherfucker i love you but you'll never know it i hate you in the morning and in the afternoon i hate you because you invited me for a drink and i had to leave the tip so fuck you"

I went back in and had a long cry. After a while, I sat at my computer. I had left the gay chat site open. A little glowing envelope indicated four missed chat messages.

"did u get my joke, ha ha"

"no hard feelings i hope"

"if u make a movie about this i'll kill you"

"just kidding. can we go on another date?"

I wasn't thinking when I chucked a bunch of things into a suitcase. No mental checklist. No calling FedEx or UPS to hold my packages, the cable provider to pause the service, or the gardener to give him the keys so my ficus wouldn't die of dehydration. None of that. I was out of there. The only exception was my Porsche. It was too conspicuous, so I made a quick call to put it into storage.

That day, I realized I was losing my mind, sinking into a quicksand of paranoia and speculation. I was permanently uncomfortable in my body, my house, my bones, the framework of my life. Yes, I had chased fame and gotten it, but now that I wasn't landing the jobs I wanted, fame was just a residual and annoying condition of my bad employment situation. That's when I realized I should've taken my mathematical hypothesis seriously. Fighting the five-year sentence was futile. I had tried to defy the math by working with Chris, and look what happened. I had flailed my limbs in the quicksand, and it only pulled me further down. I somehow had to disappear, to fade off the star radar so I could endure my misery alone. But how? Rent a hut in some remote jungle? Move to rural Canada? I could've hired a plastic surgeon to make my face unrecognizable, but that would surely be going too far. I would ask them to make me look happy.

I decided to check into a hotel, where I could hopefully obtain some privacy until I figured it out. There, I could go into a semi-coma, and I was unlikely to hurt myself or be hurt by others. I could plot my recovery and reinvention in secret, and figure out what to do with the next four years of my life, a guaranteed wasteland. And it was all because of Pinchable Cheeks.

So what if people would look for me? That was their problem.

But, because this was such a hasty plan, and because I was anxious to soak in the nearest tub, I picked the worst possible hotel. Smack downtown L.A. What an idiot.

5.

DIANE WAS RIGHT. I'm good at dreaming up the minutiae of a person's life. To truly get into character, I have to create an insane level of detail, from sexual politics and allergies to emotional colour and the colour of their ass when slapped. I have to invent it all because it's never in the script. The little details are so important. I cannot impersonate somebody until I know their worldview on cold cereal, otherwise my walk will be off. It's all connected.

I want to know what's in Chris's head, because we'll eventually have to sort stuff out together. We're going to meet. I can feel it. I have to know why he's so fucked up, even at the risk of empathizing with such a self-righteous, entitled bastard, because I want the upper hand. I'm going to imagine what he's been up to since I last saw him. I'm sure a lot of it is wrong and will simply expose the worst aspects of my paranoia. But I have nothing else to do at the moment ...

Let's say Chris Culpepper drove his silver Sebring through the security gate and into the studio parking lot, a frown on his forehead. It was sunny. If he had been in the mood to lower the convertible roof, his thinning blond hair would be fluttering and so would the collar of his blue Hawaiian shirt. But these days, he never put the top down anymore. It seemed like too much work. When he walked into the building with his Starbucks coffee, Matthew at reception greeted him, but Chris didn't smile back.

That morning, like all mornings for the past two weeks, Chris would march to the production room, throw on his ragged earphones, and listen to the same trombone sequence over and over while doing Sudoku puzzles.

The studio had had a few highly successful films over the past few years (nothing I was in.) It showed the signs of confidence. Management had expanded the facility and beefed it up. A quick chopper ride would show four shooting studios connected mall-style, a central glass atrium that housed a stand of palms, and the entire complex flanked by three parking lots, loading docks, and a helipad. If you took a golf cart down the hallways, you'd zip past a lighting studio with enough bulbs to light L.A. twice, a music studio packed with Stratocasters and Stradivariuses, walls of Fender amps and hundreds of Zildjian cymbals in eerily silent layers ascending to the ceiling, past the powder puff and sneeze of makeup, through two wings of costuming's pristine outfits used only once but all vaguely familiar. The studios themselves were like circus big tops, with cranes rigged to hold cameras and stunt people dropping like dead birds.

At the end of the day, cars started to stream out of the lot, and the crew shut the place down. They turned off lights, emptied trash cans, swept up sun-withered palm fronds from the atrium tiles, vacuumed the carpets, restocked the vending machines with cans of soda pop and sandwiches that could never die, lowered the air conditioning, made sure rooms were clear of people, locked the doors, and enabled the alarms. One section at a time, the studio machine shut down to a low hum until the following morning. It didn't always go smoothly. All it took was one workaholic to interrupt the routines of the maintenance crew, who weren't supposed to say anything when someone stayed late. It wasn't in the contract, but the unspoken pecking order was clear: never interrupt a producer, editor, gaffer, costume designer, or actor. Especially not a director. It was a venal sin to mess with anybody on deadline, because they were the ones who paid the bills, even though they were also the ones who blew the money. The maintenance crew had a joke for this, a type of sign language that they guarded closely like a gang secret: pull an imaginary bill from an imaginary wallet, then roll and smoke it. A California wildfire.

It was late when Luis pushed open the door to the editing room. He knew what he was going to find, and he was right. A mess of a man leaning back in his chair, fingers locked behind his head, forever watching the same orchestra scene in a movie with a plot so secret that nobody Luis knew had the full story. Some had bits and snatches they had overheard, and together the support staff tried to piece the film together, sequence by sequence. They filled their lunch breaks with plot holes and non-sequiturs. Conjecture led them straight into dead ends. The administration staff used their front-office proximity to sway the others into believing it was a film about a hostile takeover that the hero undid by dating someone from the attacking corporation. Maintenance had their doubts. That was just a subplot, they argued. It was a road movie about a painter following her dreams down the highway. Together the staff conspired to connect the dots in their differing theories. There were two elements they absolutely agreed on: there were wolves, and there was a killer trombonist in a key scene that was leading the director into what appeared to be a midlife crisis, if the Sudoku was any indication. Even though in reality it had nothing to fucking do with me. But I digress ...

Luis watched Chris watching the screen. As the orchestra swells to crescendo, the trombonist begins to dismantle his instrument. Methodical, cool, oblivious to his surroundings. Close-up of his hands twisting the mouthpiece off. A tiny screwdriver, tinier screws. The oboist watches, loses her place in the sheet music. The notes go to hell. The tuba leers. Flute flits. French horn tilts. Bassoon careers. Timpani comes in a half-second too late. By the time the trombonist has his lap full of brass parts, the music has turned into an orchestral bowel movement, and the cymbals clang to a crashing halt. He re-assembles some of the smaller pieces into a different shape. A narrow piece of piping attaches to a valve. The trombonist loads some screws into a brass chamber and cocks the new shape. It's a gun. He aims it and fires. A single bullet flies in slow motion to a soundtrack of a single bass note. Right through the forehead in absolute silence. The credits roll.

Luis started to sweep, the commonly accepted way of asking someone to leave. A quiet nudge. Chris, meanwhile, was lost in the sound and images. He reached forward and clicked the mouse. It froze the screen. Then he zoomed in on the actor's face until eyes filled the screen, green and clear. Chris sighed. They revealed nothing. The film was in the can and it was too late to reshoot. Could he cut the scene? He was unsure, clicking and zooming until the image was an asteroid field of giant pixels.

Now if you'll allow me a bit of masochism.

The problem with the actor was that he wasn't Pinchable Cheeks. Chris knew that getting Pinchable Cheeks was his only chance at keeping his career alive. For many in the film industry, Pinchable Cheeks was a mythical creature, his appearance the fulfillment of a prophecy. This soft-spoken, dewy-eyed hunk was the apparent link between the Hollywood system and indie cinema. People wrote about his success in his famous role as prisoner, bad older brother, and overall fuck-up, which not only had every art fag in New York City cumming in their pants, but also got him brownie points with the Oscar people. Then came a starring role with Mister Tough Guy, in a movie that made it acceptable to adapt twisted psychopathic novels for middle America. The main construction material in this bridge between worlds, as far as anyone could tell, was Pinchable Cheeks. He was the messiah of the Film Forum in New York City, the home of the cool. Chris knew that this indie-Hollywood fusion was the only way to advance his career without being forced to direct either something that got a lot of attention but was crappy, or an arty masterpiece that sank him into obscurity. He needed Pinchable Cheeks.

But the years had gone by, Pinchable Cheeks's price had risen, and he was harder to get. In desperation, Chris had sent bottles of Veuve Clicquot as overtures, but Pinchable Cheeks's management company sent them back. He asked around if anyone knew him personally. Marcia, a set designer he once hired, was rumoured to be working on a new Pinchable Cheeks project, so he asked her for an introduction. She said she would send him an email. Chris then asked Marcia if he could be cc'd, but the request must've weirded her out, because he didn't hear back from her. He sent a few apology emails and checked his inbox hourly for her reply. Nothing. It was a dead end.

Chris turned to Luis, who expected an apology and a quick exit. It was anything but.

"I've been debating whether or not to get a motorcycle. It doesn't even matter what make. But it has to have a radio loud enough to hear on the 405. Maybe a Kawasaki. You think?"

"Don't get a Kawasaki," Luis replied, not quite sure what to say.

"I don't know if you've ever ridden," Chris said, cocking his head, "but Yamahas and Harleys make too much noise. Honda has issues, and Suzukis are, well, I'm not eighteen looking for a toy anymore. What do you mean, don't get a Kawasaki? I don't know why you'd say that."

"Do you want me to explain?" Luis asked.

"First, I have another question. You've seen a lot of the footage.

Now let me ask you ... isn't the ending obvious? Wasn't it a given that he was going to shoot someone?"

This was problematic for the cleaner. The wrong word, and it could break the movie in two. He knew how important the scene was, and the fragility of the man in front of him. Poor fragile artist. The wrong suggestion, or the right suggestion taken wrong, through an accent and the haze of fatigue, and the movie could tank, financially crippling the studio until there was no money to pay someone to turn off the lights.

"Let's talk about the movie another time," Luis said. "It's late."

Chris watched as Luis emptied the wastepaper basket into a large, orange industrial garbage bag, the coffee in half-full Styrofoam cups hitting the plastic with a splash.

"Then let's talk about the Kawasaki I'm not supposed to buy."

"Okay."

"Well?"

"The radio never works."

Chris drove out of the almost empty parking lot, nodded at gate security, turned left on Melrose and took the Hollywood Freeway north.

Luis never got his apology for having to wait for Chris to leave. But I'm going to get an apology from him. He owes it to me.

The sunset cut across the city liquid orange and bright, sideways and through the holes in everything. Only the black spots of palm tree heads and the occasional shadow of a passing plane obscured the pure bath of light. The orange was deepening into a bunch of different crayon names, dying, but Chris chose not to notice. Neither will Californians acknowledge the cold that comes after sunset. We will simply turn off the air conditioning.

Chris had no particular destination in mind, but knew he didn't want to go home. Things were not going well with him and Diane. Bad blood had started to pool between them. He wondered if the movie he'd just shot had anything to do with it.

He found the Red Hot Chili Peppers on his MP3 player and blasted it. They always put him in a good mood. The conversation with Luis had unnerved him. He decided a trip through the hills would numb him sufficiently, so he took the next exit.

Soon he was testing his brakes and grip on the road, winding past yards of manicured shrubs and sweet citrus, sun-shaded driveways with cars nicer than his, Ferraris and Range Rovers with ironic yet too-precise vanity plates, swimming pools he could smell but not see because the fences were too high, mansions and cribs, security cameras, nannies pushing carriages too close to the roadside, money flaking from the eavestroughs. The problem with the hills, Chris thought, as he took a can of Pabst Blue Ribbon from the glove compartment and popped the tab, is that the neighbourhood had no barbecue culture, no meat and pineapple sizzling over charcoal, hissing to a soundtrack of lazy conversation. He could understand if people were afraid of the communal eating thing because of germs, but in the hills, it seemed to be a general dislike of friendliness.

That's when Chris thought to visit Giancarlo, one of the film's executive producers. He was somewhere up there walled in a marble palace, probably polishing off his eighth gin and tonic. I can't be sure what the man drinks, but if he's the kind of asshole I think he is, it's Bombay Sapphire. It was simply a matter of sussing the place out. Chris had seen his house once before from the driveway, about two years prior, after they had first met at a restaurant. He remembered the evening quite vividly because of what had happened to his plate.

The waiter had come to their table, recited the daily specials, and asked Chris for his order.

"We'll take the mahi-mahi," Giancarlo interjected. "With a side of venison."

"For both of you?"

"Yes," Giancarlo said.

Giancarlo was a handsome man, in a nifty Jean-Paul Gaultier blazer and crisp white shirt, his hair gelled just so. He smelled of cologne, but it wasn't overpowering, just a whiff on the collar from a week-old spray. If there was anything about Giancarlo that Chris decided to distrust, it was his sartorial understatement.

"I used to swim with these things," Giancarlo said, pointing at the fish with his knife as he forked in a mouthful. "By the way, I just want-ed to say that everybody is excited about having you on the project."

"Thanks. Yeah, it's gonna be a great film."

"Tell me your real feelings," Giancarlo said. "You're holding some-thing back."

Chris took a deep breath and swept the hair out of his face.

"I think the concept is good."

"Go on."

"That's it," Chris said and shrugged. "I guess, overall, I just want the movie to be timeless."

"Timeless. When are you going to deliver the fucking script? Is that timeless, too?"

Chris dropped his fork, mortified.

"I'm kidding, ha ha," said Giancarlo. "No, seriously, tell me how you plan to achieve that."

Chris took a swig of sangria to hide an involuntary gulp.

"Well, we could make the story and dialogue more ..."

"You want to make it surreal."

"Maybe, but ..."

"Surreal. Okay. We need to lose the audience so they can better enjoy the experience. Uproot them. Make them uncomfortable for their own good. Make them think halfway through the movie, 'Hey, this is fucked up,' but then show them how they're wrong. I understand."

"I'm not sure that's it," Chris said.

"No, that's it. We need to treat the audience like a piece of shit."

"That's not what I'm saying."

"Of course not. I'm just exaggerating, don't mind me. Can you take a joke? It's going to be fabulous ... Do you like the meal?"

"Sure."

For Chris, the movie was already surreal. It grew huge in his sleep. He would dream about it, his brain working out the math of the creative process, the plusses and minuses, constantly balancing out algebraic equations over a fulcrum. His REM sleep quickly filled with nightmares. It had a way of doing that, because all the interstices and negative space between dream sequences were a ripe invitation for decay. Like a cavity. In one of his dreams, the movie was set to shoot that day, and Chris hadn't cast any of the roles yet. He ran screaming through the set, frantically throwing on costumes and trying to memorize lines. To rescue the movie, he had to play every character. A logistical problem emerged from this terror: how to act and direct at the same time. Chris had to divide himself through an incredible act of cellular mitosis. In some occurrences of the nightmare, this tactic worked. In others, he dissolved into a puddle of plasma and the movie disappeared. He also couldn't figure out how to speak to the actors on set because his mouth was sealed over with skin. It made him frantic. There were miscues and he couldn't correct them, even by flailing his arms or crossing them in the shape of an X, in what he hoped was a universally understood "don't do that." He traced his mouth skin with a finger and it slid continuously upward, the way it does in dreams, without parameters but with too much feeling, until he realized it was his scalp extending over his entire face. In real life, baldness was slow and plodding, but in sleep it took advantage of time warps. Panicked, Chris put his ear against an offending actor's ear and screamed through it. His ear was a hole. It was possible that sound could come out of it.

As if he would ever care that much.

It was at that point in their dinner that Chris noticed something peculiar. Giancarlo was staring at Chris's plate, at his fork, at his lips closing around the food.

"Why aren't you eating?" Giancarlo asked.

"I *am* eating."

"More like pushing it around."

"I'm just not used to the texture."

"Too rubbery?" Giancarlo smiled.

The waiters suddenly cleared the room.

"Now that you mention it, yes."

Chris watched Giancarlo's smile twist into a sneer as he picked up Chris's plate and slammed it flat on the tile floor. It shattered and people jumped out of their seats. Shards of Tuscan-white china speared the supposedly substandard mahi-mahi. The dead lemon wedge landed several feet away, and the accompanying risotto was a greasy mandala that fanned out across the room. By the time Chris could register any of this, the waiter was already looming toward the table with a broom and dustpan in hand. Giancarlo was the first to speak. He wiped his hands on his napkin.

"Anyone about to make a surrealist masterpiece shouldn't be wasting their time with rubbery food, right?"

He turned to the waiter.

"Sorry about the mess. It was delicious."

With that, Giancarlo peeled three hundred-dollar bills out of his wallet, and left them on the table.

Those were in the old days. Since then, Chris had drawn an uneasy peace with Giancarlo, and learned how to negotiate around his temper. Chris crafted his emails carefully in order to lower expectations, always ending with a "we'll see how it goes," or "let's evaluate this in the light of day." They found a way to concede to each other. Plot elements revealed too early or too late, the cliché of rain versus the cliché of good weather, an actor with a dodgy background versus the suspiciously clean. Everything was on the table, because they learned how to state their opinions without offending the other. The result of such open discussion, however, is that one knew when the other was avoiding a topic. It could either be a glaring patch of electric diode-white floating in the middle of an email or a bit of heavy eye contact. There was definitely one aspect of the film that Chris was avoiding. They would eventually have to talk about it, and it would be hell.

They would have to talk about me.

But Chris knew what his defence would be. In his opinion, my behaviour was unjustifiable. He would say I had flipped out at the worst possible time, during shooting, and it was unprofessional. For his part, Chris didn't feel guilty. He believed he was upfront about the storyline being in flux, that at no time did he mislead me into thinking my character was fully defined. Didn't everyone know that was how Chris worked? He was a big enough deal for his reputation to precede him. Chris tried to think of other reasons for my anger. Midlife crisis was the most obvious culprit. He found it painful to witness a man spin apart and unravel in front of him—worse gore than any props master could dream up—even if he felt it worked for the film. But he reasoned that it was me who drove the character changes, not him. I had only myself to blame for making RR darker. Chris had merely done his job as director to adapt the film to the cast. He considered it irresponsible not to do so.

This is the bullshit story he fed Giancarlo. Snakes like him are always hiding behind evasions like this.

Chris parked the car on Beachwood Drive, his wheels turned inward to the curb. He decided to find Giancarlo's house on foot, and started walking up the incline. Couldn't be far. Chris peeked into a few of the yards through the bushes, hunting for the house. As well-tended as these properties were, California was still a wild landscape, and every manner of plant choked another in an upward race to the sun. The magnolia was in full bloom, the wisteria crept out of yards and onto the sidewalk. Deformed cactus everywhere. The cicadas were humming in harmony with a lawnmower cutting up fallen grapefruit and making the whole neighbourhood smell like a Bed Bath & Beyond. Flagstone walkways wound through rock gardens and frog ponds. There was red brick and white stucco, peeling pink-painted cement flaking off faux adobe-style guest houses that hid the real mansions from view; yes, I'll admit, the ones I've always wanted.

Chris came to a chalk-white marble house he thought looked familiar. There was a Maserati in the driveway, bugs splattered on the windshield. What did Giancarlo drive? Probably a whole fleet of vehicles. The draped windows were dark and lidded. It was worth a shot. There was a metal security gate blocking the path that led to the front door. He pressed the intercom and waited, wiping the sweat off his forehead with his wrist. The camera perched at the top of the gate caught everything.

"Can I help you?" said a voice.

The housekeeper. He froze, unsure what to say. It occurred to him that he didn't actually want to meet Giancarlo that day. It was probably a bad idea to deliver the news to him at home. It would piss him off, and Chris would be alone with him in an enclosed space. The mansion in front of him was probably big enough for an underground torture chamber, maybe even a firing wall with excellent soundproofing. So he turned around and walked away.

Chris was disappointed with his own cowardice, and he was tired and thirsty. His consolation was that the rest of the walk was downhill. He was heading toward his car, giving himself a hard time for wasting the evening, when he remembered that Nice White Teeth from the Red Hot Chili Peppers lived nearby. His house was on one of the side streets, probably accessible at the next left. Maybe Glen Green. There was no harm in taking a quick peek at the house, was there? It wouldn't be an invasion of privacy, as long as he didn't stake Nice White Teeth out or take any photos. But what if he did? What harm was there in snapping just one more exposure of a man who's been photographed millions of times? His address is publicly known and it's even on Google Earth, that geospatial celebrity homing device. How much right to privacy can the man expect, when he performs in the nude? Despite these rationalizations, Chris couldn't help but feel like a stalker. He was the only pedestrian on the street. There weren't even any parked cars. The ones that belonged there were all tucked safely in garages or behind gates. Something about the album *Californication*. The cover art features a swimming pool filled with blood-red clouds, under a sky of deep blue water. California flipped upside-down. In Chris's mind, it was well within the realm of respectable fan behaviour to wonder if this was the pool in Nice White Teeth's backyard.

Chris eventually found the sprawling rockstar villa. It had a wing he assumed was a recording studio, soundproofed with flagstone. Must be it. He hopped the security fence and skulked around to the back. But there was no visible swimming pool. No diving board, slide, swim-up bar, waterproof sound system, nothing. He stepped onto the lawn to make sure it wasn't AstroTurf hiding the pool, but the ground held firm. What a boner kill. He surmised that Google Earth must be wrong about the location.

And he was angry at himself for not trying to find Pinchable Cheeks's house instead.

Okay, maybe I'm projecting a bit.

6.

I'LL START WITH THE inside of the front door, because it's the first thing I see after dropping my bags. There's a fire information plaque riveted into the wood, indicating a non-smoking room with a capacity of twenty-five. There's a diagram of the hallway path I should follow in case of fire. It says not to panic. The peephole is huge. The wood looks like stained oak, but it's likely striated pine. I have an eye both for quality and the cheap way out. There's a plastic sign slipped over the handle that says "Shhhh." I walk backwards and stumble onto the bed. Relief always gets me in the knees. It's a delight to be allowed moments of weakness.

The ceiling is eggshell white. There is no overhead light. The tall double bed has fluffy pillows and a sandbar print comforter. I feel dubious about the goose down because the quills poke. It's nice to be high off the ground, because you never know what's crawling down there, though the carpet's not bad, as carpets go. It's wall-to-wall navy, sea to shining sea of my new fishbowl, with soft divots and other mumps of pleasure that feel good under bare feet. I'm not wearing socks; I have never liked them. They restrict creativity, as do hats. There's a writing desk with a phone, a green Tiffany-style library lamp, and an Internet port for laptops, for those who care to be connected to the sick world, for whatever sick reason. Me, I came here to get healthy. I brought my laptop, but I don't intend to use it. I don't need temptations to Google myself. I could not handle the horror of seeing the keyword suggestions, revealing what people type most often when looking for me, especially now. I can only imagine that there are thousands of results with my name and the word "failure."

I continue to study the details of my recovery room. Perpendicular to the desk is a dressing bureau with a flat-screen TV on a swivel base. Big bay windows look out onto the street sixteen floors below. I've just pulled the navy drapes shut along the ball-bearing track, including the inner chiffon lining that lets in only a minimal amount of sun. It's fabulous, that lining.

There's a hum I can hear but not feel. It's the ventilation system that controls temperature and airflow. It can blow hot air strongly. Cool air weakly. Tepid air moderately. Scorching air mildly. Freezing air torpidly. Mild air mediumly. It's like a fretless guitar. Infinite possibilities. The problem is that most will get you sick. All will circulate germs and sounds from other suites, from the kitchen and laundry rooms below, from the exhaust-filled loading docks and garbage rooms even further down in the guts of the building, and from the sewers under that, because everybody knows, and I'm not just making this up, that they never change the air filters. I think I'll just leave it off.

The paintings on the wall are most disturbing to me because they are vacuous in that kind of Monet-is-a-Degas-is-a-Rembrandt kind of way, but they're actually by a home-decor designer in New Jersey.

I'm having a hard time enjoying my new surroundings. There's already a bug in my system. All this blowing is starting to chafe my nostrils. I've become a breeding ground for bacteria. I can feel the micro-organisms multiply in my sinuses, threatening to burst out of them like spiders from an egg. The germ army emerges and launches a full-out attack on my face. Out through my over-heated Eustachian tubes to block my ears and turn my nose into a running tap. One battalion marches down my throat and into my lungs. I'm developing a cough. My ears are in a wicked state of imbalance and ringing the alarm. But I can tell it's not a cold. I start to hunt around the room for possible causes. Allergens? I've heard that adults can develop them later in life. Maybe I'm in latent bloom. And these sneezes probably echo down the halls, giving away my exact position and state of frailty. I am always so vulnerable, and it makes me sad.

I have to lick the sick. I drop to my hands and check under the bed. A rotted mouse would be germ heaven, a breeding ground for maggot flies. Nothing. So I push the bureau away from the wall hoping to find a dead carcass and the source of my misery. Only the pristine invisible line where the carpet meets wall. I inspect the drapes but they're free of mould, so scratch that. There are no balled-up tissues in the trash holding someone else's fetid mucous, only mine. What if it's coming from outside? I check the window, but it's locked. My head has started to pound. I've taken eight Advil, but the pressure just worsens. And now my throat is dry and scratchy, and swallowing hurts. Fuck! There's only one way to check for a leak or a menacing breeze: Saran Wrap. Luckily, I have a sheaf with me. I unwrap my toothbrush, straighten out the cellophane, and hold it up to the window like an idiot. This would make a great photo. He's finally lost his mind. The cellophane doesn't move. The outside is not getting in through the glass.

I'm so thankful I'm alone. I don't want anyone to see me in this state. If someone, in all innocence, were to buy me cough syrup and sinus tablets and started crushing vitamin C pills into powder and mixing it with water to make me homemade Tang, or insisted on rubbing Vicks VapoRub on my chest and feet, working the burning balm between my toes to cool me to sleep, if they brought a juicer and started pulping beets that turned my pee to blood, or fetched me SunChips, marshmallows, popcorn, and other food to comfort the sick, if they prepared a hot-water bottle at just the right temperature so as not to burn me, and if they took my temperature—if they performed all these acts of kindness, I'm afraid the cumulative effect would be devastating to me. I would surely become submissive and grow used to the doting, take their tenderness for granted or, even worse, come to see the person as a kind of saviour. Then I would melt inappropriately in my already inappropriate state of disrepair, lavish them with shameless appreciation, too many thank-yous, start talking shit they're not meant to hear, confide in them that I'm lonely, treat them like a therapist, call up relationship files from the Recycling Bin, mope, wallow, expose, disintegrate, implode, and ultimately, in the worst of all scenarios, fall for them.

Thank the fucking gods I'm alone tonight.

It must be the Gideon's Bible, which must be in the nightstand. I race over and pull open the drawer. There it is. Not the Bible, but a recent issue of *Variety* magazine. At this point, I'm prepared to make a diagnosis with all certainty, but I flip the pages anyway, knowing what I'll find.

A review. The ultimate virus.

"What to do when your mom adds you on Facebook? Just ask director WW. In his new, forgettable film *Unfriend Me*, an entire family comes of age as they grapple with technology and how it redefines their relationships. Things go awry when a grandfather tries to place a local call on the clicker and ends up ordering a cable porn movie. Michael-David plays the swarthy and incisive Dr Roberts, bent on curing the family's ills by prescribing a week without modern technology. Unfortunately, he ruins an otherwise decent film. His performance is as lukewarm as the film is vapid and his efforts at conveying empathy and pathos come off simply as cloying. Dr Roberts' self-reflective moments on the state of his own relationships alternate between maudlin and authentic, though Michael-David's for-the-cameras outbursts seem more like a personal loss of control than acting mastery. Are personal troubles starting to derail his career? The warning signs come flying at us faster than yuk-yuks about helpless teens who'd rather die than go a night without filling out a Facebook survey. We can probably blame the script, but we can also blame Michael-David for accepting such a terrible role. Or maybe we should blame a star system that continues to offer subtle roles to aging actors who only know how to ham it up. Can't wait to see what he serves up next. Not."

The reviewer forgot to insult my face. The scar over my eyebrow, the one I got falling off a stadium chair at three. The right side of my face has lax muscularity so when I smile, it looks melted and deformed. Nose blackheads. Hair starting to sprout in my ears, and worse, fuzzing the lobe. Silver amalgam fillings that cast me as a dinosaur. A receding hairline is growing the skin of my face against its will, forehead creeping up my skull. Why are people so silent about these atrocities? I should write a letter to the editor.

I'm only pretending to be upset, I think. It really was a terrible movie. Maybe WW is more to blame than Pinchable Cheeks for my current condition? Did I damn myself to obscurity years ago? Who knows.

I'm surprised the reviewer didn't notice the problems with the set design, either, especially in the teen dream sequence where the daughter is running through the digital corridors of a social network looking for her "friends," retrieving lost messages, and otherwise getting her fix. You can see the microphone boom dangling twice, and masking tape left on the floor by set designers to mark off construction zones. The "wall-to-wall" navigation was two-dimensional and stupid. The girl found her friends within minutes, so for all the effort put into physically creating this alternate reality, there was no tension and no payoff. The only satisfying part of the sequence was when someone "blocked" her by warding off friendship advances with two steel garbage can lids, makeshift shields. It could've been as big a cult smash as *Labyrinth*, but for these many loose details that destroy the magic.

Yes, I'm upset. And I don't like being sick. But I'm not going to let this review ruin my day. This is my hotel, and I will not brook being sad here. More than that, I will configure it to my liking, until I can navigate it exactly how I like. I'm going to rip open the source code, just like in the stupid Facebook movie I was in, and carpet this place with whatever patterns I need to survive. That is, of course, if I don't end up in a pile of my own mucus by the ice machine. I need to figure out a way to take better care of myself, and getting a different room seems like a good start.

I pick up the phone and dial reception.

"Hello?"

"Hi. Can I change rooms?"

"What's the trouble, Michael-David?"

I pause for a moment. I think I recognize the voice.

"That's not the name I gave you when I checked in."

"Please hold."

I tear *Variety* to shreds over the wastepaper basket, and it seems to help me breathe more easily. I get a little less angry. She comes back on the line.

"Sir?"

"Yes."

"No problem. Just come down to reception, and we'll fix it. Are you asking for an upgrade?"

"No, just another room on a different floor. I'd rather just switch up here. Do I really need to come down?"

"It would be easier. Are you sure you don't want an upgrade?"

"No. Why did you put me on hold before?" I ask. It's confrontational, but I need her to know how messed up I am. I need allies in this pile of bricks, plumbing, germs, and secrets, and it would help if one of them wore a nametag.

"I'm sure you know this is a busy place. I've always got someone on hold."

We end the call peacefully. I change into slacks and a T-shirt, and pull on a pair of Keds with tennis-white ankle socks and my Dodgers baseball cap. I pocket my room key and take the main elevator down. Nobody will recognize me wearing these horrors, so I feel safe. The elevator stops once on the third floor, and I recoil into the corner but nobody gets in. I walk through the lobby to the front desk, uncommonly cool. Must be the high of the suddenly healthy. At the front desk I place my arms on the marble countertop and smile.

"Hi. It's me."

"And you are ...?"

It's a different voice, not the woman I've just spoken with. It must've all been a trick to lure me down to the lobby. I suddenly don't feel safe anymore and start to panic. I whirl around to stare down stalkers, reviewers, and enemies hiding in the pack of German senior citizen tourists behind me, waiting to pounce. I will at least give chase. So I bolt and smack into the glass before the automatic door has time to open. There are going to be bruises. I run down the sidewalk, hail a cab, and jump in. The driver pushes me for an address but I have nowhere to go, so I tell him Hancock Park, the La Brea Tar Pits park.

When I get to the park, I find it both weird and wonderful to feel safe outside. A flock of young blond people with iPhones and lattes make a swirling landing around me, my exact geospatial position unknown in the flutter of Dolce & Gabbana chiffon. The radar's been thrown off, and I'm able to move forward undetected. On a lark, I buy a Rainbow Rocket popsicle from a bicycle vendor. The sun is shining. I've never felt so free, it seems. A Frisbee screams past me. Someone must think they're at Venice Beach. A second slower and I would've spit out the red, white, and blue sugar water to catch the Frisbee in my teeth. There's a bunch of people sprawled on benches, arguing over condo fees, talking over the guy playing "Soul to Squeeze" on acoustic guitar. I walk a little further and see tourists snapping pictures at the tar pits. There's a life-size woolly mammoth trying to crawl out of a lake of tar, reaching its trunk and tusks to kin on the shore. Probably drowning. The setup appears to be a morality play about what happens to good animals when they stray from the pack. But these fucking tourists have no idea what they're even looking at. It's clearly a story of human death. A black lake of nothingness will one day start swallowing you, and you'll probably watch it happen. Suddenly separated from the ones you love, by the time you realize you're going away, it's too late to touch them one last time. They hear your cries but cannot feel your loneliness, because they have stopped thinking about you, stopped caring. They have no choice. The hardest part is when they walk away. They will not be able to endure the sound of your last breath. Too bubbly. You know it's for the best that they pretend that you never existed. They'll shed all the memories right there at the edge of the guck and get on with their lives of avoiding tar pits. And you, dead, will be embalmed in a coat of rustproofing, your body preserved like a classic car. But nobody will recognize you. If they cut through the shell, even centuries later, they will see how the fear literally destroyed your insides, made your last few hours as pleasant as an acid bath. Something to look forward to. Anyway, the good stuff is at the bottom of the pit: wolf bones decomposing into black sludge. We won't see it for centuries.

Motion makes me visible, makes me a target, so I lie down in the shade of an oak, and stare up at the cirrus whips while the sun bakes me. I feel the grass under my hands, on my calves. I take the time to study the texture, tilt my head and full zoom on its serrations; the blade starts like a tube and then unfurls as it extends, the discoloured yellow blotches near the base. Every blade looks perfect yet is infallibly torn where you don't see it. The dried droplets of dog piss. The crinkled brown tobacco of dead shoots. This is grass, and I have never seen it before.

Not much can extract me from this heaven. But the sounds of a person running toward me is cause for alarm. I jump up and start to run. I can hear the sneakers pound the asphalt behind me, the measured rhythm of pursuit. Insistent. I knew coming to the park was a dumb mistake. I have no can of pepper spray to protect myself. With a sense of doom, I picture myself slowing down into the clutches of a superfan, who would no doubt tear hair out of my scalp for a souvenir, or worse, return me to my old life. There's nothing worse than a reminder of how successful you once were.

I run past the art museum and dodge traffic to get to the other side of the street. Then I turn around and see my pursuer. A jogger. Jogging.

When I get back to the hotel, I swap rooms on my own, without waiting for hotel management to assign me a new one. I give my suitcase a half-assed repacking. The magnetic card keys are such a scam. The software is so buggy that you can open most doors with the same key. This one takes a few tries. Later, I call reception and leave a voicemail saying what room I took on the twenty-sixth floor. I'm not sure if moving up was the best idea. Yet, I can't fathom moving closer to the street. If anything, higher up and more remote feels better. My room is identical to the last, but the nightstands are free of offending material, and the TV is an old tube model half the size. An irrational thought occurs to me: tube TVs are from a time when I was free of cameras biting me in the ass, when coverage about me was factual and not speculative. Maybe if I tuned in, the tube would broadcast me back to when things were okay. Sick fantasy, I know.

New problem to ponder: Is a jogger ever just jogging?

I am a reasonable person. There is always another side to the story, even when the storyteller is, in my opinion, an idiot and has nothing to say. Still, I will listen, legs crossed and finger thoughtfully touching the chin, eyebrows knitted together in a gesture of understanding. Yes, yes, yes, I'm wrong. No, no, no, you didn't mean it. It was an accident. Forgiveness flows from me like a fat lazy river. Take a second run. I must have misheard. You had already informed me, I just forgot. We will hug, make up, kiss it better, go out for drinks. Someone can stand me up, serve me crappy wine, make a bad fashion suggestion, or report me to the Actors Guild for breaking protocol, and I will lay down wearing a mink coat so they can stomp me in maximum comfort. I had it all coming.

But there are a few types of behaviour I don't brook. The worst is the shoulder spin. There is a certain breed of self-entitled American who feels that if they spend fifteen bucks to see a film I'm in, they have purchased the right to demand a few moments of my attention by placing a hand firmly on my shoulder from behind, which, when I'm walking at a fast clip, has the effect of spinning me around in the direction of the hand. I do not tolerate this type of rape very well. There's an intense degree of humiliation in it, because millions of people witness it. It's photographed. Pictures of my rape are sold to magazines and TV stations. It's replayed on *Entertainment Tonight* and forwarded on smartphones. Viewers probably jerk off to it in their living rooms.

I often fantasize about hurting the people who hurt me. Whenever some cokehead TMZ reporter claims they saw me shooting up in a Wendy's bathroom or shoving unlubricated Mars bars up my ass in a convenience store parking lot, my first instinct is to laugh. A few seconds later, a panorama of images flickers through my head, fanning me into rabid excitement. Javelin through the heart. Lead shavings in their coffee, the double-whammy of cut and poisoned. Lawn fertilizer planted into a casserole of baked ziti with fresh basil and parmesan. Delicioso. But these are only cartoonish ideas of retribution, and I don't take them seriously. I'm usually too embarrassed and mortified to do anything. In my timid shell, a wisp of myself and hiding from the world, I'm in no position to exact justice. I'm much more comfortable playing the victim. I figure if I do it well enough, people will finally see how much I suffer, and they'll let me fade out of the film industry. It's time to let me disappear. Yes, assisted euthanasia. Where's Dr Kevorkian when I need him? The fucker had to go and die.

But there are moments when revenge surges to clarity in my brain. It's frighteningly precise. It usually starts with me jabbing my knee into the offender's groin. Then I grab a fistful of shirt to make sure they don't get away. It's fabric of poor quality, so it will rip in my hand, and I'll be left clutching a stupid logo. Next I'll punch them in the throat, so that the knuckle on my middle finger connects with their larynx and the whole mechanism pushes in and cuts off airflow. Then, I thrust my fingers into their mouth, past caps and silver fillings. Middle, index, pinkie, and ring, they stretch my victim's cheeks and they start to breathe again. This is where the fantasy ends, because I never know what to do next. Pour in something vile and nasty? But in the moment, my imagination doesn't extend to chemicals. A carnal knowledge of the table of elements could really help unfreeze me in these bizarre tableaux.

This is the part they never show. I'd like to see television viewers jerking off to that.

I know I need to learn how to defend myself. Especially since someone is looking for me. I know this for a fact; it's not just paranoia. It's Chris.

7.

I OPEN MY HOTEL ROOM door, but it's not the bison burger with or-
chid mustard I ordered.

He has jeans with holes in the knees, long oily hair, and a huge
smile on his face. Must be around nineteen, twenty. Trouble, trouble,
trouble, trouble, trouble. I back up, but my cash-filled hand stays
thrust out. My first instinct when a cute young guy approaches me is
to give him money. An old habit, I guess.

"I left something here," he says. "I'm Tim."

"That's nice, but this is my room."

"No, I was here last night, and I left shit under the bed."

"Oh."

I back up and let him into the room. He gets down on his knees,
the faded jeans of his ass jutting in the air. Sure enough, he rolls a
skateboard out from under the bed.

Of course, skateboards now make me suspicious.

He gets back up, and his smile turns as sheepish as a sexy devil like
him can manage. Not that I'm interested. Flying elbows and knees,
hair tosses, far-fetched stories, and blowjobs that come too easily. I'm
now immune to young men throwing themselves at me, I think. But
I'm furious that the front desk let someone up to my room.

"There was a party and I got kind of wasted."

"I'm curious what you said to reception."

"I didn't say anything."

"So they just let you up here?"

"Nobody let me up here. I've been here a bunch of times, man. For
parties, I always take the service entrance."

He rolls the wheels on his skateboard with his long and gangly middle finger, finds a rusty one, and bends his head to examine it. The hair mop falls. Cute, but I need to get him out of my room, and fast. I have an idea.

"Tell me more about the service entrance."

"You pass the elevators, walk to the end of the hallway, and take the door on the left."

"Who else knows about it?"

"Just me."

"That's it?"

"Yeah, I think. I've never seen anybody else in there." He gives me a strange look, but soon brightens. "Last night's party was sick." Tim gestures to the carpet. "People were passed out all over the place. Dream Doctor was banging a chick right where you're standing."

"Sounds like a delightful time."

He laughs.

"Yeah, man. I met some really interesting people."

"I don't need to know."

"That's weird. What do you mean?"

"It means people have a right to privacy, not that you have a clue what that's about."

"Why, because I told you about Dream Doctor? That's not a problem. Everybody knows he's a slut. Privacy is, um ... not telling you who he was fucking."

We stare at each other in silence for a second as my mind races through a catalogue of Hollywood blondes.

"Listen, I was wondering if you can show me around the building."

"You mean the back ways?" Tim asks.

"Exactly."

"There's not much to know, but sure, let's go."

Perfect. I can ditch him somewhere in the hotel walls. Tim throws his skateboard wheels-down on the carpet, jumps squarely on it, and rolls to a clean stop at the front door. I have to admit, he is kind of sexy.

"Jeez, you're slow," he teases. "And put on some clothes."

"Are cargoes okay? I don't want to embarrass you."

"You can't really help that, but pants are a good start."

Tim has a frighteningly good knowledge of the building. I thought he would take me down the emergency staircase to the lobby, but instead, he whisks me through an unmarked door near the ice machine that looks more like a wall panel. We emerge into an alcove that's a landing area for a gated industrial elevator. In we go, beside a hamper full of sheets and towels. Tim locks us in, pulls a lever, and we sink with the grok and whine of gears. Standing so close to Tim, I can't tell if he smells like Downy fabric softener or if it's the laundry behind him. Through the metal grating of the door, I can see the floors whoosh by and the layers of concrete between each one. The deeper we plummet through the building unseen, the cooler it gets. I wonder how Tim knows we won't be interrupted. Housekeeping could call the elevator from any floor, and we'd be totally screwed. The kid must be reading my mind, because he flicks his long middle finger repeatedly over a switch to call my attention to it.

"See that? Out of service. You are now on a one-way ride."

"Cool," I say nervously.

Between one of the floors I see a flash of space big enough to crawl through, but it ascends out of view before I can get a better look. We hit the bottom and my heart thumps.

"We're here."

Tim opens the gate and leads the way into the basement. It's a labyrinth of ventilation equipment, water tanks, boilers, and industrial washing machines. Aphrodisiacs of detergent and natural gas. My impulse is to run, to pinball through the obstacle course and knock myself senseless with freedom, but I hang close by Tim, just in case. Funny how someone I was afraid of just a few minutes earlier is now my protector. Looks like I can't ditch him that quickly.

The uniform noise of the machines gives the illusion of silence. Tim looks me in the eye and smirks.

"So, what do you want to do down here?"

He fiddles with his skateboard. It feels like I've never been this alone with someone, but I know it's just the fumes getting to me, and maybe the destabilizing elevator ride. I don't answer him, and he takes it as a cue to start exploring. We meander through the basement past strange machinery blowing air through vents that look like shark fins, ducking drops of rusty water that make us look up. The pipes are a twisted network of tubing that subway the length of the ceiling, fat black PVC pipes and iron pipes covered with silver foil for thermal protection. Rats don't smell good when they burn, and neither do human foreheads when they connect with scalding metal, I'm guessing. Some are marked "cold," "kitchen," and "C-640-K." As Tim and I follow this labyrinth, our necks craned up like they're broken, we see pipes suddenly curve upwards, the steel joints messy with soldering lead. The pipes disappear into holes in the cement ceiling, and our eyes scan for other hot trails. I blink away tears, because a flake of rust has fallen into my left eye. Tim sees this, and his elastic teenage face squishes into a look of pity. Even in my agony I can admire his smooth features, the way the dirty-blond hair curls around his ears like fiddleheads.

"Don't rub it," he says. "Let's hope it's paint."

I freeze and obey. Tim leads me by the hand to an industrial sink, turns on the cold water, and lets it run. He stares at me.

"Well, I'm not going to wash it out for you," he says.

I cup my hands and splash the cool, bubbly water into my eyes. It dissipates the heat, but the sting remains. I turn off the tap and keep my eyes closed, leaning over the sink to recuperate while Tim pokes around through nearby boxes. I hear the clink of aluminum, and by the time I can open my eyes comfortably without the left one shutting like a pouty Venus fly trap, I see Tim sitting on the floor, his knobby knees in the air, and a collection of cans and bottles between his legs. That huge smile of his.

"Hydrochloric acid, arsenic, bleach, ammonia, boric acid. Fucking beautiful."

Tim licks his lips, and that's when I know he's crazy enough to be my friend.

"Enough to kill everybody in the hotel," he continues.

"Maybe we shouldn't be down here."

"We don't have to stay long," Tim says. "But it's good to know what they stock. Especially if you live here."

"Who told you I live here?"

"You're staying here, right? That's what I meant."

"Yes, but you said I was living here. There's a difference. I never told you that. Let's just go."

"You're free to go," he says.

What the fuck does that mean? I suddenly feel sick. A riptide of nausea. Saliva glands overproduce, inundating me on the spot. I have no choice but to swallow a mouthful of spit, and it tastes terrible. It must be the fumes of all these noxious, nauseating chemicals. I feel the glands in my armpits. At least the size of hazelnuts. Something down here is killing me. I see Tim already walking back the way we came, snaking around the laundry hampers, empty crates, and power tools. I run after him but trip over a box and fall. Fuck you, you fucking scraped-knee bastard. Need hand sanitizer a-s-a-bloody-p. Tim is gone, and I stagger. No, I'm not going to drown in my own vomit in a hotel basement. Somehow I find the service elevator waiting for me, and take it up to the twenty-sixth floor, shaking and doubled over, hands on my knees, my vision an even winter white, a spider filament of drool connecting me to the floor.

It's only after I get to my door, slide in my magnetic room key, enter, and collapse on the bathroom floor, that I realize Tim must've found another way out of the basement.

8.

THIS MORNING, I DECIDE to have breakfast in the café reserved for hotel guests on the mezzanine. It's a potentially stupid move on my part, but I take a gamble on the fact that people never see what's directly in front of them. We're trained to be biased against the obvious, so it might actually be the perfect cover. Nobody expects to see me here.

The café is a large room with twenty or so tables and a typical food spread: coffee in large thermoses, a cappuccino machine that brews but doesn't foam, croissants and Danishes, four types of cereal that shoot out of dispensers when you turn the plastic knob, a bagel and toast set-up, juices, and yogurt. There's a cheese and fruit platter that looks a day old, so I don't touch it. I stick to coffee and oranges, because I'm not terribly hungry. The TV is set to ESPN, which is fine. I can totally handle colour-commentary gripes about the Knicks and Lakers. What I *cannot* handle is seeing anything about me.

Thankfully, nobody recognizes me. The other breakfast diners appear to be tourists in familial clumps. Tall kids with their tall parents in *Beauty and the Beast* T-shirts yammering about Disneyland. Middle-aged couples who don't have much to say to each other, taking pictures of the little glass jam pots. Hey, some people are easy to please. Not my problem. There are businessmen going over meeting agendas, four laptops to a table, emailing documents to each other in all seriousness. I don't think anyone minds that I'm wearing a trillium-white terrycloth bathrobe with a blue Sheraton crest on the right breast, or that I have a dab of toothpaste on my face that I accidentally lick with every sip of orange juice, giving me thrills of mint julep. I'm invisible. This is my hotel. I should throw everybody the fuck out.

At least I have the chance to read in peace. I'm happy I thought to bring some scripts with me when I left the house. The rest can go to hell, but I love a good piece of writing. It's the story in its purest form, before it gets lost in the machine. I like to thumb the pages and scan the slug lines for interesting entry points. Why start from the beginning? If it's a good screenplay, it will be circular like a Mobius strip. The beginning will connect to the end will connect to the beginning. The middle is a waypoint where you can take a break and decide which way to go. I received a script by courier a few weeks ago, Lars von Trier type stuff, all lugubrious, with slanted light that leads you into darkness. You know what I mean. It was about a vampire winemaker who slowly introduces blood into the vintage. Characters become immortal one after the other, sipping from huge vats and fucking each other into eternity. Wonderful. I was in love with it. On top of that, I realized the film could save me from my troubles. It was the happiest morning I could remember in a while; the coffee tasted great, and the music in TV commercials made me want to dance. Hope makes you want to see the sun, open the curtains. I put on my best Alexander McQueen suit and combed gel into my hair. I sat down and called, and when they picked up, I said I'd gladly play the vampire. But there was a misunderstanding. They wanted me for a minor role with a speaking part. Who was playing the vampire? They didn't answer. I didn't even bother taking off my suit before jumping into a bucket of KFC comfort food. Turns out a high thread count is good for absorbing grease.

Today is a brand new morning, but my heartburn starts once Tim pulls the chair in front of me and sits at my table.

"You," I say.

"Don't act too excited."

"You ditched me the other day."

I sound upset, but I'm actually happy to see him.

"Dude, you were fine. It was a good thing to find your own way out."

Today he's wearing black jeans and a plaid long-sleeved shirt. It's wrinkled and smells like sweat. I shuffle my slippers and they bump into skateboard wheels.

"What are you doing here?"

"I could ask you the same question, but I don't," Tim says, giving me attitude. Those eyelashes must be two miles long. "I guess I just like it here. And you're interesting."

It's the merry-go-round. Young hustler has a tired ruse I decoded two decades ago. Maybe I even invented it. Soon enough, his knee will graze mine. If I move away, he'll split. If I hold the thigh firm, it's a clear invitation. Our interaction was scripted before we ever met. Yet, under the table, all I can feel is the skateboard, the edge of the sandpaper grip on the top of the plank against my shin. His long legs have seemingly disappeared.

"Wanna go on the roof tonight?" he asks.

"Don't you have any wild parties to attend?"

"The Doctor doesn't call me anymore. We can bring Jack Daniels and Coke up there."

"You want me to buy it, I guess?"

"If you want to, that's cool. I can pay for it."

"No, no, I insist," I reply a little too sarcastically.

I can't achieve subtlety before two cups of coffee. I take forty bucks out of my bathrobe pocket and slip it to him.

"That's really not necessary," Tim says.

"Don't be silly. See you at eight."

"It's gonna be a blast, you'll see."

After Tim leaves, I realize he's got me where he wants me. I can't ask any questions about his life, though I'm dying to know. Does he work? Go to school? Where does he live, and what frees him to spend his days with me? I can't ask him, because that would license him to probe my hot air balloon. Until pop. Can't let that happen. Maybe this arrangement is for the better. I prefer silence to lies. My immediate and most pressing worry, however, is that we didn't set a meeting place, and I'm not sure if he will remember my suite number.

I spend the afternoon nervously getting ready for our roof-exploring date. At least that's what I think it is. So I preen in the shower, fluttering my elbows to splash myself clean. The lavender body gel will at least hide the scent of my nervousness. I'm not used to spending time with people who don't know who I am. At least Tim doesn't appear to know. It would be easier for him to become a friend that way. My real friends, the ones who know me, don't have an easy time. They're scared of my fame and the unwanted exposure it can bring to them. Apparently, the most newsworthy thing aside from me cracking my teeth on a bender in a club bathroom is one of my friends doing it. Because when you're famous, the people around you become fair game for buckshot. Or investigation. I think about calling my friends, because I miss them and don't want them to worry. I could also use their advice. But I don't want to drag them into this mess. They definitely don't deserve it.

I comb my hair and wonder if this kid is attracted to the grey. From what I understand about Dad-Son politics, a number of hair colours can make me hot. This could be a money-losing proposition, but I don't mind.

At 7:55 pm, there's a knock at my door.

"Dry-cleaning."

"Ha ha," I say, and throw the door open.

But it's not Tim, it's the valet with my pressed Alexander McQueen suit.

"Oh."

I take the hanger, give him a ten, and he leaves. I can't resist trying the suit on, getting into it slowly as if crawling into bed with McQueen himself. If only I can do the same with Marjan Pejoski. I've had a crush on him ever since he let me feel up Björk's swan dress at a party. She thought I was hitting on her, but I was only trying to grope the stitching under the white wings. It was near her crotch, so easy mix-up.

Then I remember I'm going to the roof, which is probably filthy, so I change into a pair of jeans and polo shirt. I decide to see if Tim's waiting for me in the lobby. Halfway down the hall to the elevators, on the burgundy and peacock-blue paisley carpet that smells of vacuum and electricity, I run into him.

"Hey, just coming to pick you up."

"You remembered what floor?"

"I never get numbers mixed up."

We take the stairwell to the roof and emerge through the security door marked "alarm will sound if opened." There's no alarm, and if there is, we can't hear it over the city noise that ricochets up the walled avenues and spills over us, the two escapees, like pure unpasteurized joy. I should've learned from my park experience the other day not to get too excited over the empty promise of wide-open space. It's not like I can fly. I'm up here with a weirdo, and that's that.

Our playground is a sheet of gravel, punctuated by the warp and bubble of Plexiglas skylights, and hemmed in by a brick wall. It's starting to get dark, my town lights up, and so do the bubbles giving us views into the penthouse suites. I suddenly clue in that all the fun is going to be voyeuristic.

Tim has the goods. He takes me to the north edge of the building, sits on the ledge, and pours me a warm Jack and Coke in a Styrofoam cup. This kid. The drink gurgles and swooshes a few degrees warmer in my mouth before going down. This crazy Tim. I wonder what he wants. I thought I knew, but everything changes with altitude. Tim sips his own drink, takes a dollar bill out of his pocket and a black permanent marker from the booze bag. Then he writes YOU WIN on the bill.

"Watch this," he says, and flips it over the side of the building.

We both watch it sparrow down. He stares at me for a few seconds and then laughs. I can't fucking believe it. He knows what I'm thinking. It's going to land right in front of someone, and just when they think they've received a sign from the gods of capitalism, the kind of good luck you spend right away so it can breed thick and fervent, they'll realize it's unusable. A punchline on their poverty, an extreme of ambiguity, one that draws me closer to Tim. He's at least half as cruel as I am. Open the skies and let it rain more of this boy. The timing is right. His hand grazes my thigh, but he makes it look like an accident. Why don't people know when they've already won somebody? They can relax and stop trying a whole lot sooner. I'm playing him, too, but he doesn't know it yet.

"Do it again," I say. It comes out as one word with two record skips.

"I don't have any more singles."

I give Tim a ten, and he pockets it.

"This is too much. A single is more symbolic."

That's the sound of a maturity I distrust. I give him another single, and he repeats the trick from the south side of the building. Now insanity surrounds us. This time I pour him a drink, mostly Jack and very little Coke. Tim hesitates when he looks into the cup and sees the lack of suds, but he downs it in one shot. Not expecting that. We stare into the theatre of a bubble skylight, down into a dinner party. They're playing a game of charades. I didn't know people still played that. I guess it has retreated to the privacy of penthouses. It's innocence from a different world, pre-irony and pre-electricity. We take turns guessing their charades and making each other laugh. The people below applaud when we get it right, and a car honks when we get it wrong. A man passes out on the black leather sofa directly below us. His eyes are lidded half-open, though he's too wasted to see us. Tim takes a peculiar interest in this man.

"Tell me what you're thinking," I say.

"You really want to know?" Tim asks.

"I want to know."

I pour us another drink and we sit cross-legged on the gravel. Our knees touch, and neither of us moves away.

"They invited this guy because they don't like him. Maybe he fucked them over or something. Anyways, he's an asshole. So they throw a dinner party in his honour."

"How gracious," I say. "And masochistic."

"Let me finish."

"Sorry."

"So they invite him over for a really expensive bottle of wine. Like twenty bucks or something. They talk it up, where it came from, what famous person owned the bottle."

"He puts on his best suit," I interject.

"Huh?"

"I was just continuing the story."

"Whatever. So he comes over. Yeah, in a good suit, if you want. They show him the bottle and he almost cums in his pants." Tim grabs his crotch for effect, but I keep looking at his face. "They uncork it in the kitchen and bring him a full glass. It looks normal. Of course, the asshole takes a big whiff, but it's hydrochloric acid with food colouring. A few things happen in the next few seconds. First, he loses his sense of smell, then comes severe inflammation of the nose and lungs, and then the guy can't fucking breathe anymore. It's lights out. The problem is gone."

"I see."

"He was the problem," Tim adds, to make sure I get it.

Tim's smile looks absolutely insane in the light coming through the bubble, and I can see that his own story has given him a hard-on.

"You know a lot about chemicals."

"Just learning how to protect myself. You ever know a guy like that?"

"Like what?"

"Who gives you trouble."

I know better than to answer, even in my inebriated state.

"I'm tired," I say. "Let's finish this off in my room."

As we get up to go, we see the guy on the couch rouse out of his stupor. He blinks awake, and then appears to notice us. But it could just be his own reflection. Tim looks disappointed, and it strikes me that he was actually hoping the guy was dead. Tim is the real deal.

Back in the suite, we sit on the bed and polish off another round of Jack and Cokes. Like warm summer piss, but I don't mind because I'm about to get laid. My hand crawls across the bedspread and onto Tim's leg. I watch its progress and smile, until he gets up. The fingers wither.

"I'm not sure it's going to work out," he says.

"What do you mean?" I ask, heartbroken. That isn't the word, but that's how it feels.

"Can you keep up?"

"Are you serious?"

"There's a twenty-year spread between us."

"Hey, I know what I'm capable of doing. But if you're not attracted to me, that's a different story. That's fine, just tell me."

Tim swirls his cup around. There's nothing in it. This gesture says all I need to know, but he opens his mouth anyways and says something stupid.

"Listen, you're handsome."

I guess I totally misread his hard-on earlier. He was just hot for himself.

That's how Tim, the raging cock tease, the darling prick, came to live with me.

9.

CHRIS'S BODY DEALT WITH anxiety in predictable ways. Suppose his left eye would twitch. When someone cut him off on the freeway, the rhythms of his eye affected how he held the steering wheel, and it threw him all over the lane. Once he sideswiped a Mercedes and had to send an apology letter along with insurance information to, I don't know, Strawberry Bounce's eighty-year-old mom. People started calling him the granny hunter. It was an embarrassment to the studio. The social fallout gave him a case of heartburn that lasted for weeks and sent him down a spiral of Glenlivet, Rolaids, and Pepto-Bismol. A primary diet of pizza and espresso double shots didn't help his nerves or his stomach. Insomnia set in, and he drove the streets for three consecutive graveyard shifts, a messy jangle whose foot hit the gas and brakes before his brain said so. He'd visit every 7-Eleven he came across, comparing the inventory of frozen breakfast burritos and toxic hot dogs.

His nosedive into health crisis stopped the day Strawberry Bounce's mom sent him a bouquet of flowers with a short, handwritten note in bouncing indigo loops:

> Don't get too worked up about hitting an old lady, sweet-
> heart. I've been praying for an insurance claim ever since
> I got into this piece of shit. XOXO.

The note was a miracle cure, and Chris was indeed susceptible to such things. For him, Strawberry Bounce's forgiveness was the only way out of the situation. For every single fuck-up, there was a single solution, an end point on a linear plane. That's how his brain was hard-wired. This had caused him inexorable agony throughout his life. His arguments with Diane were an example of this. There was no gradual way to resolve an issue, no smooth re-entry into topics they had already discussed. Escalation was quick, and he prodded it along expertly, driving for "the answer" when no answer was possible, seeking an apology that addressed all of his feelings with a single subject, verb, and object, stomping through their West Hollywood condo and circling Diane until she made reparations she didn't intend to make, shut him up with a fake peace treaty.

"Are we done?" she asked.

"Um, not exactly."

"It's late and I'm getting hungry."

"So help me resolve this."

"Chris, there's nothing to resolve. I said I didn't like *Being John Malkovich*, and you blew up. We don't have to like the same movies."

"There's a difference between liking a film and recognizing its genius."

"Okay, it's genius."

"Do you mean that?"

"You want a resolution."

"You don't think the scene where the puppeteer takes control of John Malkovich's body is genius?"

"Um, I don't see it."

"Then why did you say it? Why did you give up so early?"

"Because it's the only way out of this fucking argument."

Diane stood over a potted cactus with oversized spines. This maddening boyfriend. She considered falling on it, harakiri style, to give Chris the horrifying choice of either plucking the wide needles out of her or leaving them in to plug the hundreds of blood spouts. His mind would split in two. She tried not to let violent images rule her thoughts. She tried to clear the blood, the cactus, the holes and think about her breathing, but she couldn't. The movies had gotten into her head, taken over her life. A non-stop battery of images and lights crowded out her most intimate thoughts. It was all Chris's fault, and if there was no end to the insanity, she'd blast an escape hole into the wall with her dear boyfriend as the gunpowder. Just like in the fucking movies.

When she first signed up for this relationship long before, when they nervously but happily inked a lease, she imagined a certain kind of life together, one of sharing. They would consult each other about troubles at work, not drag the shit home and leave it smeared all over the carpet. They would help each other through family turmoil, not use blood relations as weapons against the other. She had imagined, in retrospect, and perhaps foolishly, that when a bachelor moves in with his girlfriend, he ceases to become a child, he ceases to throw his snot balls against the wall and cry when his video game console is busted. But it had nothing to do with snot. It was about growing together. When you moved in with someone, the idea was to slowly get to know them, pick up on their foibles and peeves, the hidden quirks that form their personality. To read their source code and figure out how they were built. Only then could you form a common front against the world.

But that's not how things had turned out with Chris, and it made Diane bitter. Sure, at first she got a lot of the sharing she wanted, but she eventually figured out it was superficial. Chris would gladly help her make shopping lists, but never discussed politics with her, even during elections when the very air was charged with debate, when even strangers were engaging each other in partisan conversation.

When his grandmother died, he never cried in front of her, and he never asked the meaning of her own tears. They were evolving further and further away from each other, but there was nothing they could do. The only entry points into a person are the ones they give you. Relationship promises went unfulfilled. Shouldn't there be a punishment for people who let promises, even unspoken ones, die?

I wonder how much of Tim I will get to know. I'm addicted to mystery, and this seems to include unknowable people. I hope this does not doom me to even more loneliness, although it quite easily could.

Then there was Chris's interest in ... cuckolding sounded like such a silly word to her. A silly word for an even sillier fetish. One that betrayed his weakness and insecurity. She didn't find it attractive. She still loved him. But maybe, she told herself, she needed to leave him in order to keep loving him. Or rather, not to absolutely hate him.

She spun around to face Chris.

"I know you pick these fights because it makes you jealous—and you like that. You get off on me liking someone else's movie more than yours. Admit it."

This comment made Chris's eye twitch. It went off like a mini windshield wiper, propelling him around the room. His skin plunged red. And he got an erection.

"Is that what you want?" she continued. "Should I let Spike Jonze fuck me while we watch his superior movie? Then, when I suck his dick and he shoots his genius cum in my mouth, I'll spit it on one of your shitty little DVDs."

"That's ridiculous. You watch too much porn."

Cuckolding is a big leap, but I'm sure of it.

Diane sighed. She sat down on the black patent-leather sofa and

Chris joined her. They looked at each other. Chris pushed Diane's hair back and tucked it behind her ears. He caressed her cheek.

"I can't do this anymore," she said.

"I don't even care about the stupid movie."

"That's not true. You do. But if you want to know what's really killing our relationship, it's that you're smoking again."

A lie. But why would she waste the truth on him at this point? It would just lead to unnecessary pain.

"Not this again. Diane, it's my body."

"As long as you know what you're subjecting me to."

"I never smoke in the house."

Diane crossed her arms.

"You just don't get it, do you? I spend all day processing lung cancer data for the State of California. I don't need to do that at home, too. I swear, if I have to watch you die of cancer I'm going to fucking kill you."

A few mornings before, Chris had found himself in a smoke shop against his will—that's how he explained it to Diane. That wasn't quite accurate, because he drove there deliberately and knew the route by heart, including the shortcuts. But it was the closest to how he felt. Distant memories awakened in him with every turn of the steering wheel. The road brought him closer to the faraway thrills and tortures of nicotine, closer to the fix. He had never bought from gas stations. Chris found smoke shops more glamorous, as decrepit as they were. So, as he turned left on Fairfax, a hologram began to formulate in his throat, a composite image of the first drag on a new butt. The smell spirited up into his nose. He had quit years ago, but by the time he parked in front of the shop, his last cigarette could've been five minutes ago. Body memories die hard. The drive was synaesthesia, straight up. Every landmark was a visual trigger that illuminated mental Kodachrome close-ups of the speckled orange of the filter, the crackle of first light, the curl of gunmetal blue, the lungs reclining into passivity, welcoming their slow destruction and becoming weaker with every puff as the cherry glowed closer, the world slowing down so he could enjoy the last haul of tar and who knew what else. Chris's body knew the chemical composition of Camel Lights, but he did not. I'm not sure about the brand, but Chris seems too fancy to smoke GPC and too much of a Democrat for Winston.

When he walked into the store and reached for his wallet, he was shaking with resistance but powerless to fight these old forces. Through a specific set of life circumstances, the memory had come back too strongly. There was nothing to do but give in.

When he met Diane, Chris had been nervous about going out with a state public health administrator. On their first date, he had tried to hide his habit. They went for Vietnamese food, and then to see *Terminator* 2. Chris was jonesing halfway into the flick and carved two craters into his thighs with his fingernails. By the time they hit the Dairy Queen drive-thru for a banana split, Diane had figured it out.

"You smoke, don't you?"

"How did you know?"

"Give me a break. Your car smells like an ashtray. And you chewed the Coke straw until it disintegrated."

"Oh. Do you mind if I have one? Will it bother you?"

"It's your body."

Chris pushed the dash lighter in and reached for his pack. She stopped his hand midway and steadied the tremble.

"Wait," she said.

Diane gave Chris the first long kiss of their many happy years together. It was a memory his body still remembered, but in a different part of his brain, far from the symphonic striking of a match, or the tapping of a butt on his watch to pack in the flavour. Diane locked the memory into him with her smoke-free tongue. Clean, pure, and new.

"I'm not going to kiss you after you smoke. Just saying."

Chris didn't smoke at all that night. He smoked for the first few months of their relationship, but then quit with her help. He went on the patch, and it was torture. It's the mouth that craves nicotine, not the arm. He quickly pronounced it an inferior toxin delivery system, not worth the exorbitant price. But he soon began to experiment with the patch, finding different spots on his body that could accelerate the osmosis, give him a more potent nicotine high. It was a Thursday night miracle when he discovered his spine, a mainline to his pleasure centres. He cut the patch into three strips, pressed the adhesive side to the skin between vertebrae, leaned back into a chair giving it all his weight, and fucked himself with poison. It was the shit, almost as good as the orgasms that Diane gave him, but not quite.

Chris was on the patch six months longer than recommended. When he called the hotline on the back of the box for advice, they hung up on him, no doubt fearing a lawsuit. There were studies linking misuse of the nicotine patch to heart attacks. One day, he forgot to wear a patch, like someone would forget to put a band-aid on his ankle when wearing new shoes. Chris was in the middle of a film project, overloaded with work. Attending financing meetings and casting calls, distracted by negotiations. He was shocked when he realized he'd gone a week without a patch. Hadn't even missed the chemical high.

He was nicotine-free for several years, but the monkey always finds you. This new nicotine pull was precipitated by a nasty turn of events.

10.

Giancarlo finally agreed to meet Chris. Let's say that this time, Chris chose the restaurant. It was an Asian fusion place on Canon Drive in Beverly Hills, famous for its grilled urchin salad. It's disorienting when your lettuce appears to have spikes, and that's exactly the feeling he wanted Giancarlo to have when he broke the news to him: confusion. Rather than explode into fury, Giancarlo would be boggled in a haze of kelp nectar and sea cucumber ravioli. In fact, Chris bet that it would be so unnerving for him to be unable to differentiate an animal from a vegetable, to be so helpless before round globs and serrated shells with leafy attachments, that he would forget about the bad news altogether.

It was, at least, a nice fantasy. But a nice fantasy for whom? For Chris or for me? I'm starting to get confused. I feel like the actor in *Being John Malkovich*, once he has full control of his human puppet. There are now two sets of everything: opinions, neurons, removed tonsils. Even worse, I may be starting to feel for my aggressor. I can't afford a case of the Stockholm Syndrome, sympathy for the devil. What I want is a full blubbering apology, an acknowledgment of wrongs, while he grovels on the floor and looks me in the eye. And I don't want to seek it. He has to come to me of his own volition. The problem is that the more understanding of him I gain, the less likely I think the apology is.

Chris slicked his hair back, fastened two buttons on his white dress shirt, and then unbuttoned them immediately. He looked at his reflection in the avant-garde chrome napkin holder and gritted his teeth. A mess. Two women at a neighbouring booth stared at him and conferred in whispers. Chris wanted to visit the bathroom to fix himself, but just then Giancarlo walked in, spotted him, and joined him at the table.

"Nice place," Giancarlo said, motioning with his head to the neon octopus clock on the wall.

"Let's order," Chris said.

They each perused the menu and picked out relatively conservative meals. The safety of a tomato sauce smothering a recognizable animal, names they could pronounce. Chris had picked out his meal thirty minutes before Giancarlo arrived, so he had time to dwell on the anxiety chipping away at him, the same thought over and over: the movie is done, and it's going to be fucking cancelled. Cancelled. Cancelled. Cancelled. Cancelled. Cancelled. The finality thudded. This was the black hole of directors' nightmares. You work for years on a project, only for it to disappear into a vault, into a stack of contractual clauses, into the void. Years of life lost. Chris had met directors who had lost their movies. To him, they behaved like parents whose children had died painful deaths from leukemia. They were hollow, unable to feel anything, unable to laugh, or they forced themselves to laugh at jokes just to hide the emptiness. These were once high-functioning people able to juggle multi-coast lives, jetting east and west so often that their bodies absorbed the three-hour time difference, biological clocks reconditioned to adjust automatically at 38,000 feet. It always happens in the plane, just before take-off, before the flight-safety video says to turn off all electronic devices. The director gets one last phone call. It's sugar-coated and hedged, but the message comes through clearly. A whole world has vanished because of competition, buyout, or pure financial strategy. The studio might have shot the movie just so nobody else could, or so the writer couldn't wiggle out of the option. A green light with no intention of release. The director's life is destroyed before the plane takes off, because they imagine all the phone calls they will have to make, the mountain of condolences waiting in their inbox, the years they'll have to wait for another script that good. It will be a decade before they visit Sundance again. And they have six hours strapped in a seat to think about it.

I wish the movie could get cancelled.

"Barnacle in pesto pomodoro," the waiter said, bringing the plates. "And this is the Tandoori Bolognese. Enjoy."

The waiter walked off.

"If you don't like it, we can go somewhere else," Chris said.

"I'm sure it's fantastic. What did you want to talk about?"

There was no room on Chris's side of the cushioned booth for him to drop under the table and run out into the street, which is what he wanted to do.

"He's missing."

Giancarlo said nothing.

They ate in silence. Rather, they listened to each other's epic slurping and clanking. A conversation, if you read between the lip smacks. Chris had nothing to decode, because Giancarlo appeared to be enjoying his meal. Only the sounds of satisfaction. He wiped his mouth with the aquamarine napkin. On it, the tomato sauce looked like blood.

"His agent called me," Chris continued, hopeful that the discussion would not go that badly.

"Let's talk about something else. Hey, the weirdest thing happened the other day. I saw a guy who looked just like you."

"Oh yeah?"

"Yeah, he was sexy like you. You know you're a handsome mother-fucker, right?"

"Uh ... Okay."

"I mean, look at you. Tell me one woman who wouldn't want to fuck those bones. You're a god. All confidence. Probably have a nice cock, too. Good head, big knob. Anyways, enough of that gay shit. So I saw this guy almost as handsome as you are. You know where?"

"Where."

"Outside my house."

"That's weird."

"Do you know what else?"

"What."

Chris could feel himself getting lost in a labyrinth. Giancarlo was a movable wall popping up at every turn, directing him where to go. There was only one way out of the maze, and he feared it was straight into a sausage grinder.

"He was looking into my house. My wife was upstairs getting changed. We don't have any curtains right now because the decorator is redoing them."

Chris swallowed hard. His mouth was empty.

"But he was walking," Giancarlo continued. "That's how I knew it wasn't you. You may be an Adonis, but no offence, I can't see you making it up into the hills without a car. Too bad, though. You're a handsome fuck."

Giancarlo gave him a look and clinked wine glasses. The waiter cleared their plates. Chris had barely touched his meal. Dessert was deep-fried balls of pistachio ice cream on a single plate with two silver teaspoons. Two shots of double espresso with tubes of raw brown sugar.

"But you're concerned, so let's talk. Missing, you say?"

"He hasn't been seen in a week."

"Only a week?"

"That's a long time for someone like him."

"Who told you this?"

"His agent."

"I know people who avoid their agents for months. The actor doesn't want to work, but the agent needs money. It's as old as this city. Tell me what you mean by missing."

"I mean that he's missed appointments, isn't answering email or phone calls, and when they went to his house, nobody was there."

"Travelling."

"Giancarlo, don't you think he has an iPhone?"

"This ice cream is good. I love pistachio. Question. Did you bring me here thinking I wouldn't like it?"

"I don't know how to answer that question. You're not taking me seriously. I just gave you bad news, and you act like it's nothing."

"Relax. Let's go for a drive."

Chris felt weird watching his Sebring disappear in the passenger side window as they pulled out of the parking lot. Giancarlo drove through the city and into the hills, not speaking. He turned onto Mulholland Drive, and soon the lighted city sparkled through the trees. It was a balmy summer night, but Chris's toes and fingertips were frozen.

Hollywood is all timing. You turn and smile just in time for the camera, and you're tomorrow's cover girl. Cover the camera lens just in time, and the life lines on your palm will be all over TMZ. Stop into the right party and you'll meet the voice coach whose sister is Johnny Mathis's personal assistant, and you'll get the autograph you've wanted your whole life. Tap the brakes prematurely, brace for the crash, and fill out insurance papers with Penelope Cruz. Disaster strikes only once for the lucky. Be the first to bang out a message of support for a shark attack, deadly earthquake, or miscarriage of justice, and your soundbite will be the one they play over and over.

Unless you're forty.

It goes without saying that you should honour the gods of timing if you want good things to happen to you. You should never miss your own premiere. But the movie was coming out in less than a month, and I was indeed missing. Yes, lost in the middle of L.A. Toronto would be a farce. Word would spread and people would speculate. Who misses their own premiere? And why? The scenarios played out in Chris's mind. Chris didn't think of the most obvious gossip. The director is an asshole and drove him off the set. He's impossible to work with. Or, the movie is a lemon, and the actor doesn't want to be associated with it. The worst film in decades, the worst since *Throw Momma from the Train*. That has to be it. Refund, please. A confirmed flop.

Instead, Chris was so desperate that he was willing to consider a sunnier side of media speculation. Did Michael-David escape to a hidden tropical locale to celebrate his new flick? Was he with some young thing, tipping back Mai Tais served in Swarovski-rimmed coconuts? Was it part of the marketing campaign to keep the actor undercover until opening night, when he would jump out of a stretch Humvee onto the red carpet and into the adoring flash? Quite possibly. It's time to look for him. www.letsfindMichael-David.com. www.Michael-Davidsinmycloset.com. www.whereishe.com. www. thatsnotjohnnycashthatsMichael-Davidonatrain.com. The mystery would propel it to the front pages. Websites would track sightings of me and post grainy iPhone shots that visitors sent in. There would be no way to filter fake news of me being found. It would be a publicist's ultimate fantasy. A studio couldn't buy that kind of hysteria, and it would make the film a box office smash.

Or, they could assume I was dead. The truth is that the media has been praying for another *Dark Knight*, for an actor to mix up his prescriptions in a state of frazzle and die during editing. It's a dirty truth that nobody likes to talk about.

There was a likelier scenario. I think Chris knew the truth would eventually come out. I would turn up in the fray, and with microphones in my face, explain the details of my disappearance, methodically and at great length, reading from a sheet of paper as if giving a police statement. I would stare straight into the camera and give the reason. It would be more than Chris could bear.

"It didn't turn out like he said it would."

Chris is a one-solution type of guy. He would have to shoot me.

Funny how quickly a prop gun can change hands.

Giancarlo pulled onto the side of the road and got out. Chris followed. The city was a glowing grid of light with multiple vanishing points, full of people lost in plain sight. Giancarlo spoke.

"He's the killer. The killer can't be missing."

"I'm not sure what to do."

"Find him before the media hears about this. I bet you think it's good publicity, but it's not."

"I never said that."

"You and types like you don't know a single fucking thing about how the business works. So listen to me. Find the fucker. And don't even think about cutting him. It would destroy the seventh symphony completely. I have a question. How did you know I like pistachio ice cream?"

That question, like many of the best in Hollywood, echoed down into the city and went unanswered.

11.

I DON'T MIND THAT the kid lives with me. He's not a serious offender as far as roommates go. Sure, Tim always splashes the toilet rim when he takes a piss, and he never closes the door. But I find it sexy. He always takes a mountain of fruit from the Continental breakfast trough, and then lets it rot in the room until we're inhaling fruit flies. Yes, so four hundred-dollar bills were missing from my wallet when I checked it this morning, but so what? He left a note saying that he had to get "emergency supplies" he hoped "we would never have to use." Perfectly understandable. He steals the covers in his sleep. It's annoying, but it's also cute how he bunches it between his legs. I'm pretty sure that with a little education, I can turn Tim into a gentleman. I should take him to J. Crew for pants without holes.

I recently came out of the shower to find Tim watching Mulholland Drive on TV. That scared me. I'm in danger if he knows what I think about. He appears so often in my thoughts. But what freaked me out even more, for reasons you will later understand, is when he ordered Zelda through the TV's paid gaming features. I could not take my eyes off how he manipulated the joystick in his hot, skinny hands.

He goes shopping all the time, but not for clothes. A typical trip of his will yield a bag of unknown goodies, rattling and poking through the plastic, emitting weird smells. The whiff of trouble in his purchases. One time I worked up the courage to rifle through a mystery bag, so I stuck my hand in without looking and got poked by metal prongs. Part of me didn't want to know. What I first thought were candy rockets turned out to be radio transistors when I dumped the contents on the bed to study them. They looked like caterpillars with

Lifesaver stripes and metal antennae. A soldering iron and a coil of lead, deceptively light. Licking the lead would probably be less dangerous than spending another night with Tim, given the strangeness of his wares. There was a hypothesis brewing in some unused recess of my brain marked, "It had better not be fucking true." To confirm my theory, I'd have to get out my laptop and perform a Google search, but I fear the keywords are so heavy and suggestive that they would trigger a series of red-flagged emails sent to the Department of Homeland Security, who would, in mere seconds, mobilize a task force to locate and detain me. Another way would be to check my credit card statement. I'd surely find a vendor on some terror watch list. But that's just my imagination running wild. I would probably just end up abusing my time at the computer. I would succumb to curiosity and commit a small act of everyday suicide: type my name into the search field and watch the results fill the screen, my name in bold, bannered and raped, blogged and spun, hyped and with foreign suffixes glommed on, embedded into advertising spam, riding Trojan horses, and all in lowercase. I'd type in a misspelling hoping for the comfort of fewer results, but everybody misspells these days. Fuck it. So, in a desperate attempt to end the nightmare, I'd try swallowing the rest of Tim's purchases, the innocuous-looking but fatal LED lights, green resistors that looked like alfalfa sprouts, miniature power supplies small enough to scrape down an adult human throat but large enough to short out a nervous system.

I don't really care if he's building a doomsday machine. I'm more fixated on the ease with which he Frisbees my credit card around town. I should tell him to stick to cash, because otherwise he's flashing my name around the city, and that's dangerous to my privacy and my mental health. Either way, why is he so comfortable taking money when we're not having sex? I'm not imposing any conditions on him, but you'd think a hustler type would be more sensitive to the dynamics of exchange. He seems too confident, too secure about his place around here. Something about it bugs me. I'm starting to suspect that he sees himself as my protector, but the idea is ridiculous. How can he know who to protect me from? Even if I explained, it would take him a while to grasp the complexity of the forces that have driven me into hiding. My enemies are mostly invisible, and probably quite good at evading over-obvious boys.

On the other hand, Tim might be wondering why I keep him around when he's not giving me sex. Good point, and I'm not entirely sure I have the answer. Maybe it's the anonymity. He doesn't ask questions and doesn't give a crap what I do, which is a good start. It's so rare for me to be able to interact with someone without my fame getting in the way. I get to say what I actually think and feel, and it's not filtered through the cogs and sprockets of the fame machine. It makes me feel ten years younger.

And Tim's a great TV companion. I wasn't expecting that. We lie in bed flipping through the channels together, taking turns to veto the drivel that slides by endlessly. I hold the clicker. When he taps my wrist, it means "change." It seems a harmless enough intimacy to allow, this symbiosis. At the very least, our collaboration rescues us from watching many poorly written sitcoms. I click again, wait, but Tim's hand, hovering, never comes down. It's a nature show about roving wolf packs. The candid footage is incredible: fighting, fucking, chewing carrion like bubble gum, sleeping with tails curled around chilly snouts. The wolves never look into the camera, even by accident. Good stealth or good editing, one of the two. The narrator describes the situation. We're witnessing a "disfellowshipping" in progress. The pack is ostracizing one of its own, slowly but methodically cutting it out of the group. The camera catches every moment of this relationship surgery. It's a male, beautiful and silver-tipped, and he's no longer welcome. The stages are clear, the voice says, but the reasons are not. Unlikely that it's territorial, or even a mate dispute. Wolves don't fuck with sex. The narrator points out that it must be something subtle such as "differing views of the immediate future," which, if it's true, is a brand-new insight that will forever change things for the wolf-watching community. If wolves can visualize time on a continuum, then they could be planning all kinds of scary stuff.

The footage is heartbreaking. The narrator calls the silver-tipped male the "shunnee," as if pronouncing a name the pack has bestowed. The pack closes in around a deer carcass in a tight circle to lock the shunnee out. Their nonchalance is their cruelty. The shunnee approaches, hungry and sniffing, and tries to wedge his lithe body into the circle. It doesn't work. The circle swells, pretending not to notice him. Fur puffs out, bristles like porcupine quills. There is no room for him, and he does not dine. Later, the pack shames the shunnee by gathering to watch him pick through the bare bones. Loop and slash, the wet tongue comes up empty. The camera pans the circle of content shunners, always a circle. They sit in judgment. At night, they drive him out into the blizzard, taking turns to guard the circle of heat when he inevitably returns. Howling, sad, cold, and starving. Unacceptably thin. Night after day they do this. The parents train the pups to shun, and they are instant experts. Cute little black noses made for snubbing.

Wolves are not lonely like people think, but they know how to create loneliness like no other beast besides humans. This is what the narrator says, and he's probably right.

Tim taps my wrist, but not to change the channel. He gets up and goes to the bathroom, unfortunately removing his long, slender legs from my line of sight just below the TV screen. He lingers in the bathroom doorway, as if knowing his limbs will draw my gaze.

"I saw a wolf camping once," he says.

"Really? The wolf was camping?"

"Thanks for correcting my English, man."

"Did you get close to it?"

"You can say that. It was hunting us. We could hear it sniffing around the tent. We had to poison it, but it didn't die right away, that's the thing. It made a last run at us on two legs. Fuckin' amazing."

He must see the horror on my face.

"Dude, I'm fucking with you."

"Asshole," I say.

He disappears and shuts the door.

I keep flipping the channels, aware that it's only a matter of time. My instincts are right because I soon see myself on the screen, giving an interview. Yes, a self-immolation. My eyebrow scar is in high definition. The mouth speaks, answering the questions. I appear strong, but will soon fall apart. I can guarantee it. It's a wonder this performance doesn't make me sick. Am I getting used to the public shame? Do I feed off my own misery? I wouldn't be surprised. Whatever the case, I don't change the channel.

"Do you ever get attached to your roles?" asks the interviewer.

"I'm not sure that's something I would know. I enjoy my work, if that's what you're asking."

"Okay ... Here's a question from one of our viewers—just making it clear it's not from me."

"Let's have it."

"You don't mind?"

"We'll see what the question is."

"All right. Are you seeing anybody?"

"Um, wow."

"Yes, this is what people want to know, apparently. And they'd rather hear it from you."

"I guess that's a good thing ... so, seeing anybody? No, not right now."

"But you were? I wonder if we'll find out who the lucky ... duck was."

"Yes, I wonder."

"Well Michael-David, this is the point when, as a decent journalist, I should stop being nosy."

"Ha."

"You see, I'd love to do that, but I'm getting a feeling from you. Maybe a feeling that you have more to say, and I should stop being so decent."

"If you're asking me about ..."

"I'm not asking anything, Michael-David. Not a single thing."

Tim comes out of the bathroom and sees me. The TV. He's going to find out who I am, and whatever beautiful mess we've created is going to evaporate. But we can't keep living this way. Tim's going to find out anyway. He flinches and I know it's care, not fear. And that's what I'm afraid of.

"Turn that shit off," he says.

"I can't."

"Michael-David. Give me the fucking clicker."

Has he known all along?

"Leave me alone."

"I'm pretty sure you can afford therapy. You don't have to do this to yourself."

"Let me watch."

Tim shakes his head, puts on some clothes, and leaves the suite. Now it's just me and the interviewer.

"Only if you're comfortable," the interviewer says.

"Yes."

How bad can the question be? I've forgotten what comes next.

"Is there any bad blood between you and Pinchable Cheeks? I mean, some might say that he's been upstaging you for years."

I turn the TV off.

12.

I CAN'T SLEEP. TIM is a tosser and turner. He'll implicate me in his nightmares by twisting the sheets until my feet are tangled and ankles hog-tied. Sometimes, during his full-body revolutions, his skinny forearm will flop onto my stomach and I'll wake with a start. The arm will lie there, and I'll study the veins, the straw fuzz. Then his pale feet will nuzzle my calf, toes bending to a faint tickle. I'll pull away and retreat to my side of the bed, but his extremities will find a way to creep back and touch me. In my fantasy, this is all on purpose. But I know it's not, and that's why it's maddening. And these movements don't conform to the dreams I know he has.

Tim told me about a recurring nightmare he wants to get rid of. It always starts with him as a puppy born in a barn to a family of golden retrievers. His first impressions as a newborn puppy are the bales of dirty hay, the monstrous horses nearby, and the sopping tongues of his parents. They constantly lick dust, manure, and bits of hay off him, smoothing his ears down, pushing the fur first the wrong way and then the right. Every time they speak to him, it's in a different language. This is very confusing to Tim the puppy. Then the farmer comes into the barn and presses him against a chopping block. When the farmer smiles, cigarette ashes rain down into Tim's eyes. He tries to blink them away. The axe falls and chops his right ear off. He struggles and squeals, his little eyes wet with pain and fear, darting between the farmer and his helpless, broken parents. The left ear is next. The puppy is warm in his own blood. Tim once resorted to taping down his ears at night to ward off the dream, but it didn't work. The farmer started unwinding the duct tape and using it to fasten Tim's puppy mouth shut.

Of course, it freaks me out. I wonder how Tim would react if I told him the source of his dream: Chris's script. It's twisted. How can I transmit dreams without dreaming them? Do I mouth the script in my sleep? If Tim knew Chris was responsible for his nightmares, he would definitely want revenge. This kid lying beside me is a dark entity. And he might actually have the opportunity. The strange part about trying to tell Chris's story, to the best of my imagination and clairvoyant abilities, is that I can actually feel him getting closer to me. It could be paranoia on my part, but he could find me in a matter of days. Not necessarily to apologize. He might come to inflict more wounds. But Tim and I could also cause him a lot of damage.

Eventually, Tim will sigh and turn over onto his stomach.

We've upgraded to the penthouse without telling anybody. The front desk will eventually figure it out. We have a living room, dining room, bedroom, and an office area that looks out over a terrace. That's the best part. We have a balcony the size of a tennis court, a sun room with swivelling glass panels for weather control. The railing is lined with flowering hibiscus trees in clay pots, cushioned lawn chairs, and a foosball table. There's a coffee table with coffee-table books about designer homes by the sea. It's a good space to share with a stranger who probably has as many enemies as I do. Plenty of wicker to chuck around, if it comes to that.

Tim is making busy in the kitchen, measuring liquids and storing them in the freezer. Phosgene, chlorine, and its cousin chloropicrin. Choking agents, as Tim explained to me earlier. He's wearing a gas mask. I don't ask him what's for dinner.

"I hate this place," he says. It comes out muffled through the mask. "I hate it because there's no reason to leave."

"I can give you a few reasons to move out."

"Ha ha. Hey, by the way, tonight we start to become immune."

"How does that work?"

"Practice."

"You obviously know what you're doing."

"Actually, I don't. This is military shit. But we can't let anyone know we have this stuff."

"Are you sure this is safe?"

Tim doesn't answer. He seems taller than normal, so I look at his feet. He's been standing on the skateboard the whole time, wheeling himself back and forth between the fridge and the counter with discreet, noiseless heel pushes. It occurs to me I'm living with a young David Koresh. Am I financing a one-boy terror cell? Am I going to die in a haze of chemical glory with a hustler-scientist? This penthouse is the Branch Davidian compound where we'll camp out until doomsday, when our enemies will race up the elevators and staircases with the singular goal of destroying us, but we'll be ready. We will calmly follow the plan. First, we exterminate them. Next, we stand on the balcony with arms outstretched and helicopter to heaven. It has been prophesied that Angelinos will bear witness. These standoffs seem so ridiculous until you find yourself preparing for one. Then they make perfect sense. Sad, though, how a kid with a skateboard is the best I can muster for personal security.

"I'm lonely," Tim says, looking directly at me.

I can see it in his eyes, not as a lack, but as a presence. Telling him this could reassure him, but it could also come off as doltish. Instead, I say nothing. I could wrap my arms around him, but that could be dangerous. I wonder what control I'd have over my hands on the bony ribbing, thumb tips plunging to consume more, separating meat from cartilage, him from himself. I would want to feel his heart, and that could be very misleading to someone you only met a few weeks ago.

I lie down on the sofa for a nap and dream of Tim as a puppy, his ears bloody and chopped, unable to hear anything his parents bark at him. I sleep fitfully, too aware of my position on the sofa. My arm falls asleep and then bristles with a wave of needles. I wake up, and feel the first hit as a uvula tickle. Then I start coughing. It's not like any other cough I've had before; this is a full deep choke. I expel the air violently in bursts but can't inhale. My lungs want oxygen but my throat denies it. In this sudden, inexplicable battle of impulses, my body is suffocating itself. Fuck. The pressure creates an instant head-ache. I burn from the inside out. Lose more air but can't replace it. This is a horrible way to die. My face feels bludgeoned, busted. I'm streaming tears, so when I open my eyes to see, I think the patio door isn't too far, not far, so I run, I fall and run and smash into furniture, hope I smash through the glass because I'm. Quickly. Emptying. And. Not. Filling. Back. Up. Cough, cough, help!

Then I see my rescuer standing by the patio door. Tim unlatches it and throws it open just as I aim my shoulder to break the glass. The momentum throws me into a judo roll and I clatter against the flimsy wicker furniture, sending it flying. I keep coughing, but this time it's new air. I take bigger and bigger breaths, ripping off my shirt so I can feel the proper functioning of my diaphragm once more. It's all so unceremonious.

Tim removes his gas mask. It's Canadian army surplus. Don't ask me how I know this. It's either the near-death experience or spending too much time chatting with costume people between takes. For a split second, I picture Belgians watching the Canadian soldiers march through town to end the Nazi occupation. Some are on foot, and some ride in tanks, waving and giving cheery salutes. And then there's Tim on his skateboard.

"How was the war?" he asks.

Is he for real? Maybe this is still a dream and I'm supposed to die.

"How was my fucking nap?" I scream. "You almost killed me!"

"You're exaggerating. Things just went a bit wonky in the kitchen. You were never in danger, really."

I cough up a gob of phlegm onto the patio. It smells like swimming pool.

"Why didn't you open the door sooner?"

Tim raps his fingernails against the clunky metal box at the end of the mask's breathing tubes, which presumably holds the filter.

"You're not fucking serious," I say. "I was your guinea pig."

"You're seeing it the wrong way. Fine, so when I talked about building immunity, that wasn't the right word. Chlorine is too toxic to become immune to."

Tim takes out a pack of Marlboro menthols and lights one up. I've never seen him smoke before.

"It's more about knowing what to expect," he continues. "And knowing how people will react in different situations."

Tim takes a haul off the cigarette and gives me a look that vacuum sucks the space between us. He sounds too mature, too calculated, and it makes me suspicious. There's something he's not telling me. And he's taken more control than I'm used to giving up. I need some leverage.

"Who are you running from?"

Tim ignores my question and just stares ahead.

"Well?"

"You didn't say anything when I said I was lonely."

"Was I supposed to?"

"Never mind."

"Wait a minute. Were you trying to get back at me just now?"

"Don't be stupid. I lost track of the measurements. About the other thing, it's just that when someone says they're lonely, it's an opening into a conversation. You chose not to take that opening."

"And your point?"

"Michael-David, do you want me to fucking leave?"

We stare at each other. Tim, despite all of his efforts to remain detached, will end up revealing his insecurity. Michael-David, his body fighting noxious gas and feeling defensive, will show the many black facets of his heartlessness. Oldest script in the fucking world.

"I was going to ask you about the loneliness," I say.

"Oh, yeah? When?"

"Eventually. When the timing was better."

"That sounds like an excuse. I bet a guy like you uses it a lot."

"What the hell? What's a guy like me?"

Tim shrugs, and starts walking away.

We are each other's counterweights. So when he goes silent, the change in air pressure sucks my blood to the surface of my skin and makes it dance hard and crazy in my neck, the veins all pulsing toward him. I want to slap him until he talks. I jump up and punch a hole high into the wall, and when I pull my fist out, it rains crumbled plaster and flecks of white paint onto his pretty head. It's almost beautiful, like a snowglobe scene. Tim looks scared. I can't hold back.

"Hey, hey, hey, I want you to fucking explain yourself! You've been making these sly comments for weeks now, and I'm sick of it."

"Fine. Just don't hit me."

"I would never do that."

"And don't be upset with me."

"Out with it."

"Well ... it seems you're afraid to know when someone feels the same way as you."

I move closer and he flinches. I'm starting to relax a bit. I massage my sore knuckles. Tim realizes I simply want to pick the debris out of his hair. He stands still while I ferret everything out. I notice how he's slouching so I can have easier access. It's a considerate gesture.

It's time for a good talk. Tim goes out to get Chinese food for us, and when he returns we eat on the terrace, talking for real in the fresh air over plum sauce. Open for the first time, that's how it feels. It's a relief. Tim recognized me when we first met, but decided to be discreet and respect my privacy. He didn't want to be, in his words, "just another slobbering fan." I tell him I appreciate that quality in a young man, and that I don't consider it dishonest. I suck the meat off a spicy duck wing. I've recovered from the choking gas with only occasional hacking. Tim finally asks all of the questions he has about film, and I answer openly. I tell him about the films of mine I like, the ones I despise, and the roles I'll never get because of my age, my limbo. He questions the math a bit, but his reasoning is weak. I tell him about my stalkers, and he's surprised to hear how crazy they are. It's particularly embarrassing to him that they're mostly young men. He knows this makes him suspect, so I reassure him: when stalkers get you in bed, they rape you. That's not exactly what's going on here. Tim laughs. He compliments my chest, and I remind him of my age. He laughs again. We soon sink into a deeper conversation. What it means to be lonely. I tell him about my failed loves, the boyfriends and girlfriends, the rings and abandoned promises. Why do we need to make promises, rather than just give the most we can every day? I explain how I've given up on dating. I also admit to using celebrity as an excuse not to trust people, to absolve myself of taking responsibility for friendship. It's a form of masochism I use to punish myself for staying in a job I don't like. What do I want to do? I'm glad Tim asks. Travel the world to see its architecture and hear its quiet spaces. To revert from being a brand back to being a person. To enjoy a few years of unscrutinized experiences. Start a blog. Find a boyfriend. But I'll probably end up acting in a film about all of the above and will have to settle for the simulacra of real life, as usual. Tim laughs so hard he starts to choke.

Over to his side of loneliness. Sex killed most of his best friendships. Whenever he met someone he liked as a friend, he'd try to fuck them, but not because he wanted to turn them into a boyfriend. He thought sex would bring them closer. His horniness was a genuine curiosity about the other person, a desire to learn more. So, to deepen his platonic relationships, Tim became a master seducer at seventeen. Precocious, talented with buttonholes and zippers. Tim explains how it doesn't take long to find the sweet spot on a friend's body. Grazing it will always produce a sound, revealing the path to a heavier connection. He figured out only too late that sex made people "weird." With sex, you make it past the outside wall, but then you can hit an inner barrier and you're suddenly trapped inside someone. You can't get in or out. The ultimate loneliness. After a few trips to this purgatory, Tim swore off sex altogether. It took his quasi-boyfriend Jason, who he was "sort of seeing," weeks to convince him to fuck; he begged Tim wearing only an bath towel. Jason assured Tim that nothing would change, and he cited his past relationships to prove his point. Was he sure? Absolutely. Jason advised him to have some faith. Tim relented and got naked. Within days, the friendship turned like a sour stomach. "I told you so" is no consolation under those circumstances. Tim said that's when he lost trust not in people, but in trust. He continued to have sex in a few of these altered relationships. Sometimes it made sense for him to take money. Cash defined expectations that the friendships couldn't. It was a reliable mediator. And it was "fucking hot" for someone Tim knew to pay him twenty bucks for the privilege of licking his balls.

That kind of talk always awakens my dick. Is he opening a door to something more?

Tim reveals that he owes money. Thousands. But he doesn't give the circumstances. Perhaps it's for non-fulfillment of a sexual contract. I hold a few questions back. What did he spend so much money on? He doesn't appear to have a drug problem. Smokes are pricey, but that appears to be a new development. That's the thing with Tim. He relates his experiences as if they span years, but it's actually weeks and months. His newness is invigorating.

We go inside. It's almost time for another exploration of the building. Up next are the garbage chutes. Tim bends over to lace up his lime-green Pumas. I inch closer. When he straightens, I'm in his face. I grab his shoulders to feel the width of the body I want to fuck so badly. Can't take it anymore. Tim's breath is hot. The trace of cigarette smoke isn't that disgusting coming through his beautiful lips. I want to tell him we should have sex, that the timing is right and that he'd enjoy it. I could grab his crotch to get things going. He has just tried to kill me, one of the most intimate things a person can do. Sex would not be a huge stretch. But the kid totally derails me.

"Are you prepared to kill someone if you have to?" he asks.

"Um, I don't know."

"I want you to think about it."

Tim and I sneak into the third-floor hallway, because it's the hall-way with the least amount of foot traffic. We peer into the garbage chute through a release door he has unscrewed. Sometimes trash bags clog the pipe and you have to fish them out. Every floor has one of these escape hatches. Tim disappears inside. His legs seem longer as I watch them slither down the chute. Soon the square tube of gal-vanized metal has swallowed him completely and he's just a clank-ing echo. Clang, plink, bang. I join him, but it's not easy because I'm a heftier man. The edges of the hatch are sharp, so I untuck my shirt and grab the fabric like a glove so I don't get cut by the metal edges. Inside, it smells surprisingly clean. If no trash gets caught, it's a straight, uncomplicated drop into the compactor. I ponder Tim's question. I suppose I could kill someone if they were trying to kill me. But I'd have to close my eyes for sure. The descent is slow. Sections of the chute are joined with rivets every few feet, and I use them like rungs on a ladder. The rivets are only half an inch thick, so I have to press my sneakers hard against the metal to avoid slipping. We're free of the outside world, so the discomfort is a small price to pay. I don't hear him anymore. Tim has shimmied away somewhere below me.

"Tim?"

"Turn your flashlight on." His voice reverberates with a metallic zing.

As we literally crawl down the hotel's ass, I imagine what it would be like to crawl up Tim's. But I have to abandon that beautiful fantasy, because I don't know where we are. Where's the trash compactor? We must've reached the basement, but I don't see it.

Unless we've passed the basement and the building goes even deeper in the ground.

13.

UNSEEN FORCES BEGAN to churn around Chris, casting a gloom. The signs were impossible for him to ignore, and the more vague they were, the more upsetting. He would get phone calls about email threads that he'd missed. There had been some discussions. Why was he excluded? Chris was informed that he had taken too much leeway with the film, made poor casting decisions. There must have been a way to avoid this. He asked for more information. Who had sent the emails? Not at liberty to say. It's delicate because the media could get involved. He asked if he should personally find the fucker, as Giancarlo had told him to do. That was a good idea, though they would have to clear it through Legal first. Technically, he was a missing person. But off the record, do what you have to do. What does that mean? Click.

Chris went to the studio one morning but left before lunch because the air was suffocating. Thick with leftover gossip. The maintenance crew had by then figured out the plot of the film and was quite satisfied with their discovery, but conjecture about the new troubles was wild.

Luis: There was a sex scandal involving Chris and Giancarlo's wife.

Rosa: The child actor died when posing with his wolf co-star during a promotional photo shoot for a World Wildlife Conservation Fund calendar. It bit off his arm at the shoulder and he bled to death. The photographer caught it all while shooting January's page.

Phil: The movie was a piece of crap.

Chester: Chris Culpepper was a Scientologist and felt the film was sending unacceptably dangerous levels of thetan out into the world.

Nobody could agree on what was going wrong, so they mashed their hypotheses together. It was commonly accepted that the maintenance crew, given their physical proximity to the production, were the closest to the truth. They overheard all of the secret conversations, right? Their version was the one that stuck: Chris was going through a midlife crisis and a self-destructive rampage. It spread quickly through the company, which quickly became a toxic environment for Chris. Colleagues either avoided eye contact with him altogether, or they were super-friendly, which made him even more suspicious.

But it wasn't the gossip that bothered him the most. It was the last paragraph of an email he had read. He was in cc.

"As you can all understand, it's quite complicated. We need to think about all the options, including finding a co-director for final cut. We're counting on everybody to be reasonable about this."

Chris got into his Sebring and left the studio lot for the last time.

The smoke shop owner remembered him. She had long chestnut hair that hadn't lost its Daisy Duke shine. Camel Lights hard pack and matches, please. Outside, he tapped the box on his palm to settle any loose tobacco strands. He unwrapped the cellophane, flipped the lid, and grabbed a butt in his fingertips. This was the rhythm. It slid out so willingly. He rolled the stick between his lips, and reached into his pocket for the matches. His lungs had been tar-free and breathing easy for five years.

That cigarette fucked them something good.

14.

DIANE LEFT CHRIS A few weeks later. Outwardly, the reason was smoking. Of course, there were many other things she didn't tell him about. Yes, he had a right to know. She would have told him had he asked the right questions. But he didn't ask.

The breakup ruined him. Chris became a shabby haze. Shots of Glenlivet flowed until he was buying three bottles a week. He later downgraded to Johnnie Walker. The drinking was unkind to his complexion, widening his cheek pores into large red whorls. He was between projects, so he played video games all day. Diane didn't fare well either. She started to lose concentration at work and made some serious filing errors that cost thousands of dollars and delayed state health projects for months. She spilled tea on her keyboard more than once, forgot friends' birthdays, and stopped taking care of her hair. It hurt when people noticed.

The problem was time. They had put eight years into the relationship. Their lives were too integrated for a clean break, so their separation was a prolonged and painful dislocation. Diane decided to move out. For every bookshelf, cupboard, and closet, they needed two moving boxes side-by-side. Chris. Diane. Chris. That's Diane's. Whose is this? You gave it to me. Are you sure? Read the gift card: I love you. Far too agonizing to read, just take it. No, I never wanted it anyways. Every box would end in tears.

Chris, now thoroughly dissolved into just another substandard component of Johnnie Walker, was too numbed to care. Now on the twenty-fifth level of *The Legend of Zelda: Twilight Princess*, he kept playing right through moving day, while the movers picked up furniture and boxes and plants around him, creating holes in his environment. Oblivious to all of this, Chris reached the thirtieth level by the time they took the last box. There was no goodbye, not even for Diane. She took a last look around the place, empty except for a TV, a couch, and a man with his back to her. She dropped her keys on the floor and closed the door.

A week later, Chris realized he was alone. He was sweeping the dust out of the hole where the fridge had been, and he found a picture of Diane. He cried for the first time since she'd left. It is unbearable that the person you spent almost a decade with doesn't like your personality. Diane had never said so, but Chris felt it. The good times were a charade of happiness. The ultimate betrayal. He tore up the letters that she'd written to him over the years, the congratulatory card when he got his first big gig, condolences when his favourite aunt died. One day he found dried flowers pressed into a book commemorating an afternoon they'd spent together happily lost in a national park. He crinkled the brittle petals into the toilet bowl and flushed.

When he left home one morning for a junk-food run, he had no intentions of visiting the surveillance store, but it was on his way. Its late-night cable TV commercial had always made him laugh. They used a riff on a classic Hall & Oates song. "Private eyes are watching you, they see your every move." Californians have every reason to spy on each other, the ad said.

When Chris walked into the store, he expected to see detectives huddled in private rooms where they could inspect electronics in secrecy. He was disappointed with its drabness and supermarket ambiance. Every sort of shabby American was thumbing cheap-looking products in plastic shell casings on the racks. There were bugged ashtrays for suspected flings, software to secretly read someone's unread emails, hand-held sonar that can penetrate walls, and teddy bears with nanny cams hidden in the belly-button. Many of the surveillance products were oblong: a microscopic camera on a bendable stick for peering around corners, a Jewish mesusa that digitally recorded comings and goings with a timestamp, and ultraviolet light wands for detecting semen on bed sheets. "Our Biggest Seller," a handwritten sign proclaimed. The wand had a bulbous head and a slender handle with ribbing. The place could've been a sex shop.

"Can I help you?"

The guy behind the counter had a seashell-white moustache, one half stained with nicotine.

"Just looking."

"We have some new video surveillance gear. Military grade."

"Wow, that sounds heavy."

"It's not heavy. Let me tell you something," the old guy said, patting his leather vest, a reflex looking for smokes and coming up empty. "One of these days, you're going to meet somebody. They'll seem real nice, and you'll become friends. Beer, bowling, fucking the same chicks, the works. One day, you'll have them over and they'll make a strange comment. They might compliment your double gas barbecue in all light-heartedness. It's single gas so you don't say anything, you just take it graciously. They got it wrong. No big deal, right? Am I right?"

Chris figured he should say something.

"Right."

"Wrong, my man. You've never been more wrong in your life. Because you used to have a double gas grill, but not anymore. That's when you look your friend in the peepers"—the shopkeeper stared hard at Chris, the fury of his next point illuminating his eyes with a bright smudge—"and bang, it'll zap you like 220 volts. He knows everything about your life. Where you've lived, what cereal you eat, if you pick out the marshmallows, who you've fucked, who's fucked you over, if you sniff your own armpits, if you piss in the sink, if you cheat on taxes, if you whack off in a monkey suit thinking no one's looking. Ha. It's all there. You've been putting on a royally messed-up show. Meanwhile, you don't have a shred of background on him. Well, guess what? That's your fault."

"Is this supposed to make me feel better about shopping here?"

"Let me know if you need any help."

Chris bought a Hitachi digital video camera that came with a tele-photo zoom. He left it in the box for a week. It sat on his kitchen table. He stared at the packaging while eating every takeout meal, reading the German and Italian instructions, scrutinizing them for evidence that he was a bad person. Finding none, he eventually opened the box.

The next week, he was parked in his car down the block from Diane's new place, filming her in her new backyard. Good thing the neighbours didn't have bushes and he had a clean view through the zoom lens. This was not despicable, he reasoned. His motives were pure. All he wanted to know was whether or not she was happy. Yes, Chris knew he should've been spending that time staking out my place instead, but that could wait a few days. Watching an empty house would be boring.

Chris and his new telephoto zoom were trying to detect and cap-ture moments of relaxation in Diane's body language, the droop of a muscle that he formerly knew as tense. She was tanning in a bikini that showed off her nipples. He stared into the screen, and watched Diane occasionally shift her limbs on the deck chair and rub sun-screen over her bare arms and legs. The ripples in her calf muscles revealed nothing for the moment, but he would later review the footage. She languidly turned the pages of a novel. The plot appeared to sink into her peacefully. She eventually took a nap. This was pointless. It was also masochistic. Chris realized the further torture it would lead to, the endless hours of watching and re-watching the video, and the low, lonely point of masturbating to the departed. The sicko in him wanted her to be jumping around the yard happily doing cartwheels so he could feel a deeper hurt.

And yet, he couldn't stop filming. Questions unspooled in his mind: did she take the garbage out on time? That had always been Chris's responsibility. Diane was clueless about trash and recycling. Maybe it festered in the kitchen until maggots grew. How did she decorate her new bedroom?

Who was she fucking?

Chris was sure that if he studied the footage long enough, those stolen moments of his ex making a new life, all of his questions would be answered. But, in the end, he decided he didn't want to know. He erased the footage one evening by recording Sunday Night Football over it, a warm case of beer in his lap.

15.

THE ONLY GOOD THING about the clog and choke of the Santa Monica Freeway was that it gave Chris time to read.

At home, he was always too distracted to get more than a few paragraphs into a novel. Invariably, something a character said would make him think about work, he'd start checking email, which grew more and more poisonous by the day, and it would kill his reading session. MSN was the worst. He'd get sucked into one-line exchanges that lasted for hours, taking endless tangents, until he realized he and his chatting partner had nothing left to say to each other. If he tried to return to his novel, the dialogue would start to resemble MSN ping pong, and he'd heave the book across the empty room. Empty, because he had failed to buy new furniture after Diane left.

So the Sebring became his library. He trained himself to see the trail of red brake lights, even in daylight. It started far up ahead, illuminating one car at a time like an airport runway, until it reached him. By the time Chris had to tap the brakes, he would already have pulled a volume from the makeshift bookshelf on the back seat. He kept an Amazon Kindle in the elastic sling under the sun visor when he needed to impress someone, but this felt more like a paper media type of day.

He picked up a book on celebrity look-alikes. There were photos of stars on the left side, their doppelgängers on the right. Some of the resemblances were uncanny. Mick Jagger had a counterpart who mastered his pout and strut. There was a young man posing as k.d. lang. One would think Liza Minnelli was beyond imitation, but that wasn't the case. The world was full of charming kooks who loved to be photographed. There was no shortage of up-and-coming Seattle grunge rockers who could fool the average easterner that they were Kurt Cobain by playing the entire Unplugged album with a sweaty mop of hair obscuring their vision. And here was Nice White Teeth. There was Nice White Teeth again. Chris was disappointed to learn that greatness could be replicated so easily.

Sure, it was a picture book, but there was accompanying text under the photos. Some of it got his mind racing while he was practically stalled in traffic.

What's in a famous face? A face can only be famous if it looks like everyone you know. Let's concoct the fatal mix to test this theory out (see diagram on opposite page). How strange that he has your professor's chin and the dimples of your first crush. The eyes? That guy you always see at the supermarket. The face also looks like every place you've ever been. A nose that slopes between Rome and Greece but never picks a side. The eyebrows float away like a Micronesian archipelago, yet their apex is the Pyramid of Khufu. Notice the cheeks that sink as deep as Lake Baikal. This man could be anybody. But he's not (see next page).

"He's Cary Grant!"

The traffic started moving again so Chris closed the book. He took Exit 5, drove a few blocks, and parked in front of the surveillance store. He decided to gift himself a new doodad he'd need for the task ahead. He walked in and saw the old guy at the counter.

"The Hitachi is nice, but it's commercial gear," Chris said.

The shopkeeper's eyes lit up.

"Glad you're coming to your senses. What are you looking for in particular?"

"Not sure."

"If you want to be one of my regulars, cut the horseshit. I'll treat you right, with a special discount on Thursdays for being a friend of the store. It ain't Thursday, but seeing as we just had this talk, we can make it a comfortable fifteen percent."

Chris reached for his pack of cigarettes, and then let his hand fall away. A phantom, aimless stab to comfort himself.

"Okay," Chris said. "I need a GPS tracking device." He leaned in closer over the counter. "To put on someone's car."

The front door beeped and another customer came in. He hovered near the entrance, examining the closest gadgets. The shopkeeper watched him intently, unblinking. Chris looked around surreptitiously for security cameras but couldn't see any.

They don't recognize the new customer, but I have a pretty good idea who it was.

"I think it's time to talk military," the shopkeeper said, shifting his gaze from the new customer to Chris.

"Shoot."

He reached for something on a shelf behind him and placed it on the scratched glass countertop between them. To Chris, it looked like a small pipe bomb. Wordlessly, the man demonstrated how it worked by removing a film off an adhesive strip and sticking it to the underside of the glass. It held firm like an octopus sucker. Then Chris saw concealed in the old guy's hand a remote device with a flashing light that gave his skin a red glow. He pressed a button and showed Chris numbers on the tiny LED screen: 34.071738 -118.40035.

"Latitude and longitude within two feet. You can find a mouse cock in a Walmart."

"I'll take it ... Do you want to know why I need it?"

The shopkeeper pursed his lips, which gave his smoky cheeks a wry twist.

"I can see I've taught you nothing. Manage your own destiny. I just provide the tools to help you get there. But be aware that this thing comes from Customs and Border Protection. If they ever find it on you ... well, let's not talk about that. But you have to understand that confidentiality runs both ways. You catch?"

Under different circumstances, Chris would've felt weird slinking around Diane's green Volvo under cover of night, hissing at tetchy neighbourhood cats so they wouldn't meow the neighbours awake and blow his cover. But this was different. Lying on the grease mat under the car, his every movement—from removing the film from the adhesive strip to patting the GPS tracker for luck—felt supremely justified. After all, Chris had seen something transpire months ago, at a dinner party when he was drunk but not wasted enough to mistake what he saw: Diane in close quarters with me. It drove him crazy to think about the interaction. What intimacies we shared over the finger food. Diane complained to me about her ridiculous, inebriated boyfriend and I consoled her, reminding her that not all men are that thoughtless. She moved closer and we shared a joke, a phone number, a fantasy. She'd put her arms around me! Weekend getaway in plain sight where nobody could see. Maximum discretion. Now that Chris and Diane had broken up, it would continue to be discreet because I was in hiding.

Yes, of course. He was bang-on. I kept Diane tucked under the bed along with Tim's skateboard.

Chris wondered if he had seen the signs all along, if my attitude had changed radically mid-shoot because maybe I was reacting to the updates Diane was feeding me about her relationship woes, how bad

Chris was to her. The most insidious love triangles had invisible dotted lines. It was all beginning to make sense to Chris. Of course, Diane would use smoking as an excuse. The alternative was admitting to an affair, a betrayal. Maybe she had even secretly coaxed Chris back to tobacco, breaking cigarette sticks into his pillowcase where nicotine could invade his dreams and life anew. L.A. was a town where people used dreams against each other.

He wondered if he would strangle us both, should this dark, nasty theory prove true. If he should strangle us face-to-face, so Diane and I could stare into each other's eyes, catch the fading glow and see who was sorrier.

The sex. Under the car in the dark, it drove Chris crazy to imagine me fucking Diane clandestinely in their old bedroom, ejaculating movie star semen into his girlfriend, then wiping it out of her and sliding two sticky fingers into her mouth. Taste the transgression.

Chris unzipped under the car and grabbed his cock.

The things Diane must've said. He'll never find out because he's not smart enough. Fuck me like a real man, not like my sissy boyfriend. What a strong touch for a change. Your dick puts his to shame and makes me happy like his never could. His tiny balls, ha ha, like chickpeas. You should totally make him your slut, have him polish the shaft that's going to pound his girlfriend deeper than she's ever felt it. Then my sissy boyfriend is going to get on his knees and clean you up, puppy-lick you good and obedient. And he's going to fucking love it.

Chris choked out his cuckold orgasm with a yell, his vision turning milkshake white.

And in that moment, he realized he didn't know who he wanted to find more: Diane or me.

It turned out it didn't matter. A few days later, when Chris gathered the courage to click the button on the GPS remote, the red light flashed, and it gave him the coordinates 34.052304 -118.255591.

My hotel, according to a Google search. A truly interesting point in the cosmos.

Finding one of us meant finding both.

But he's going to be wrong. He's going to come here and find nothing, and he'll be so fucking sorry.

16.

I EMERGE FROM THE shower clean but mussed. The heat always makes my skin red and blotchy, so I try not to touch myself under the pulsing stream. I look so silly covered in my own fingerprints.

Tim is soaking the drapes in different chemicals, performing patch tests at different heights. Formaldehyde. Formic acid. Nicotine. I watch him all day, dabbing swaths of fabric with a paintbrush. The material either disintegrates, changes colour, or singes and smokes. Sometimes all of these reactions. The drapes are pulled closed, so the sun shines through the holes of his more successful experiments. Or least successful, as the case may be. I can't tell whether or not he's aiming for maximum destruction. Here's a Chiclet-size square of linen stained yellow like a smoker's tooth.

These are experiments, but they're also turn-ons that get me bothered in the craziest way. By this point, I want to fill his body with sperm. Tim's showing off how dangerous he can be to my enemies. He must know I find personal security hotter than McQueen, no? These games are going to send me over the rail. Today he's wearing the waistband of his jeans so low it hangs below his bubble butt. A mushroom of boxer shorts. Sagging, I think it's called. God, the tour I would give his ass. I'm not a porn actor, but I would still walk out of the shower and into a sex scene. Quintessential bathroom floozy.

Tim drops his paintbrush and walks over to me. I try to ignore how he side-winded as if avoiding an invisible obstacle. Camera sight line? I'm hopelessly paranoid.

He wraps his arms around me, grabbing my wrists behind my back. His hair falls through the V-neck of my bathrobe and onto my chest.

He presses into my semi as if to locate it. Tim grows me expertly by pressing his lips to my ear and modulating air pressure at different levels. Sweet suction. Then he turns around and grinds his butt cheeks into my crotch. On the back of his neck, the patch of smooth skin I can see through the blond fop, my mind projects an image of heaven: our spines twisted and wrenched in pleasure. Broken, even.

"Do you want to fuck me?"

I've waited weeks for these words, but they're so painful to hear.

If the industry has ruined sex for me, my suspicions about Tim compound the problem. He spends almost as much time in the suite as I do. I trust him at ninety-five percent. Five percent is friendly but ambivalent and is willing to consider that Tim has planted mini-cams around the hotel room to record a sex tape worth about $300,000 US, a figure that's a rough algorithm of what a Britney-in-a-limo vulva shot can fetch. I've never been photographed naked, as far as I know. Has Tim been buying surveillance equipment with the money I give him, and is he now finally ready to use it on me? Ergo, the recent and prolific ass shows?

I can trust people, that's not the problem. The trick is knowing when someone has earned $300,000 worth of my trust.

Otherwise, why this sudden change in Tim's policy? I'm not his type. Maybe he's starting to feel the imbalance of our financial arrangement too acutely. The pressure of dealing with a creditor. I wonder if he thinks I've been counting the money I throw his way. Why can't this generation of pretty young men just accept money guilt-free? They imagine strings where there are none. Have I been placing undue pressure on him? I don't believe so. I use cash mindlessly. Mostly, I like to see the colour green move across the room. You could call it performance art.

In case this is not all imagined, I figure out a way to make the footage less valuable. I'll keep my clothes on, and Tim will be the star attraction. Not only would that reduce the tape's value, but it would make Tim reconsider putting it up for sale. The drawback is that I'll have to be more patient about getting off. .

"I want to see you jack yourself."

"Why don't you do it for me?"

"You do it," I say firmly, with an air of sexual authority. My inner daddy is coming out.

He looks at me, as if searching for clues on how to drag me to bed. But I'm still slippery from my cocoa-espresso shower scrub. There's nothing for him to grab onto. Ha! I'm becoming a better hustler in my middle age. Tim walks over to the sofa and plops down. He spreads his legs wide. A stretch of faded denim from one armrest to the other. There's a hole in his crotch that I've been ignoring for weeks, and now it's all I can see. The plum-size gash is left of his zipper, and a testicle spills through. It's the carelessness that gets me hot, if you'd like to know. Deeper into the denim hole, I can see the thick blond bush. A few scraggles poke out. It looks like carelessness, but it must take skill and practice to manipulate his boxers that way without ever taking his eyes off me. He's fucking me with that smirk.

The unzip is a slow tease of his long fingers. Tim lifts his legs in the air and shucks his jeans, one pant leg at a time. Then he kicks his boxers off. Socks stay on. Wow. He's blessed with a beautiful slab of meat. It's swollen with veins and hangs to the right. His foreskin droops at least an inch off the edge of his thigh, red and abused. His scrotum is loose and flops down his ass crack, his raphe. That descending ridge is dark and razor sharp. Blond fur everywhere, browning into nether corners. Overall, his cock looks insolent. He clenches his butt. He'll probably leave skid marks, but it's worth it. Under pressure, his dick twitches to life. He pinches his nips. As his shaft lengthens, the head pushes through the foreskin, smoothing out the only wrinkles on his body. Slit glistens with pre-cum. Then Tim starts jacking. I'm convinced there's nothing more beautiful than watching a young man slap his dick around. All of his muscles tense up, the leg muscles turn into planks, the biceps into tennis balls, and the deltoids give him triangles you've never seen. Parts of his fist turn eyeball white. He can't keep from closing his eyes tightly, and his abs give a washboard show. But it's the dick I care about. As his body temperature rises, his scrotum loosens. The slaps echo in the chicken-skin hollow between his legs. Between pumps, I see flashes of his asshole. Then his balls suddenly crawl up into his dick, and his hand goes furious. He spurts in arcs over his chest and stomach, heaving it out like poison. Beautiful semen. What kind of white is this? For once I have no words. The smile is killer. It's all boyish pride: look what I made.

I consider joining him to take what's mine. If a hidden camera is recording all of this, I would only ruin the purity of Tim's performance, such a great cinematic moment. But then it hits me. A sex tape would give my career such a fantastic kick in the ass, that I'd be back in the inside circle, the subject of dating rumours and magazine photo spreads. I'd be able to get the best table at Fontana's again, right under Miss Piggy, that sweet pig. I'd get any part I wanted, and my worries would be over. I can't believe I didn't think of this sooner. I start to *pray* that there's a hidden camera catching all of this.

I walk over to Tim, slide two fingers through his cum, and stick them in his mouth, past the teeth until I touch tonsils, paint them slippery with my fingertips. Tim represses a gag and his eyes shoot open, enlightened by his own taste. Then I take a taste myself. He's bleach, but it's sweet. Then I lube his asshole with cum. So many things to teach him. I leave him for a moment to get condoms from my suitcase, and when I come back, he's worked up another hard-on, no miracle. My own semi is all veins, growing when I open the condom packet because I'm conditioned to certain smells, an obedient Pavlov dog. The smell of condom latex always makes me so swollen it hurts, because it's a precursor to sex, to the scent of Tim's asshole after I wet the curly brown mouse hair with spit. I swirl it until goosebumps dimple his cheeks on either side of my face and I bark approval up into him, my voice muted but strong, reverberating up his body. He's on my taste buds. I explore Tim like he's the hotel. I'm going to get emotional doing this because it always makes me think of the straight men, not that Tim's straight, but who knows. There are billions of men who will never get their assholes rimmed. They'll never feel the exquisite squirm of an admiring tongue, curious and exploring ever further. Muscular but gentle, and always wet. They'll never feel the tingle of someone worshipping them from below, a hundred times more intimate than a blowjob. While rimming Tim I think of this, of the men forced to go through life feeling their asses are underappreciated, those perfect globes, hairy and smooth, round and tomato-shaped, rank and sweaty, a summary of who they are. All in denim gift wrap. Ignored for no other reason than they forgot to ask someone. In frustration, these men will resort to bombing and killing each other, blowing each other's asses to shreds. This makes me so sad, because all it takes is a little lick.

By the time I put the condom on, I'm a bawling mess. I've completely forgotten that this is the most glorious thing that has happened to me in months. Tim is giving me the strangest look. Not knowing the back-story, he just thinks I'm in love with his asshole. Well, he's not entirely wrong.

17.

I HATE AFTERNOON NAPS. Not only do they mess with your circadian rhythm, but you can wake up from a beautiful dream into a nightmarish situation.

Let me start with the dream. I was sharing a hotel suite with forty wolves. This very hotel, but a much bigger space with room to run around. It was in the sub-basement, a place I think I discovered with Tim. In the dream? I don't know. It had cold cement walls, musty corners filled with spiders, and a damp ceiling with limestone stalactites jutting down. Unreal calcium formations turned the floor into a moonscape.

The wolves and I would wrestle all day and feast on raw carcasses at night. Rabbit, horse, greyhound, the usual. I salivated buckets with the best of them. Fights would break out sporadically over the heftier bones. Marrow held high currency. It was delicious. They taught me how to suck it out, and they clapped their paws when I learned to do it quickly enough. Red blood cells were filling. I felt safe with these beasts around, but more than that, I felt kinship. Even love, we can go that far. They regularly gave me a good smell-through, nuzzling me to the ground and licking my eyelids shut. When they disciplined me by nipping my hind quarters, I felt the affection more than the sting. I stared into those ice-green eyes and got lost. This was friendship built out of muscles, tendons, sinews, hunger, trust, and fur. These animals were proud of my greying chest hair, and they almost eviscerated me when I tried to shave it off. It was that kind of relationship.

This is my afternoon dream. I wake up too soon and roll out of bed. By the time I reach the doorway, I've decided that this penthouse suite will no longer do. Fear has propelled me upwards, higher into the building. The great disappointment is that I have not made headway in discovering my true self. Seclusion has been useless, except to spike my paranoia to a permanent high drone. The problem is that I have no escape from the inchoate noise of my brain, no perspective from the madness I inflict on myself. The fact is that I'm crazier than anyone I know, and it's the fucked-upness of the world that keeps me sane, stops me from folding in on myself origami-style, like a dollar bill, and fluttering naked off the top of a tall building, say, a hotel downtown, and splattering in front of some lost Angelino waiting for a sign from heaven, who would, with sweet serendipity, read the words written in black marker across my stomach, YOU WIN, and wonder for years afterwards what the heck it meant for them.

It's time for that to end, to move down closer to the street. I need the people, the noise, the disinformation, the hype, the speculation, my stalkers, anonymous and strange-smelling fan mail, the devotion, the threats, the unwanted photographs, the pulled hair, every split end of normal public life. Got to get it all back. If all that stuff is waiting for me just outside these hotel doors, then I need a ground-level suite where I can prepare myself, primp and spruce, trim nostril and ear hair, shower, iron some Alexander McQueen, slick my eyebrows back, and meet it all with accepting glory. I will finally understand and forgive and be grateful, because I cannot stand a minute longer of myself in such close quarters. Hotel rooms are too small to be living in with ogres.

I will forgive everyone but Chris.

I throw on some jeans, a dress shirt, and my Dodgers cap, and head down to the lobby to make the arrangements. It's the only reliable way, because reception has stopped answering my phone calls. Tim's not around, so he can't do it for me.

Strange. When I get to reception, I see Diane waiting there. This can only be trouble. I look around nervously. She's wearing a suit and carrying a briefcase. She looks shocked to see me.

"Hi," I say.

"Wow. This is incredible. Do you know how many people are looking for you right now? The premiere is in a few days. Why are you ..." she says looking around, "in a tourist hotel? In downtown L.A.?"

"It's a long story. Mostly involves sacrificing small animals."

"Seriously."

"Yes. And some career second-guessing."

"But why are you—whatever works for you. It's none of my business."

"What are you doing here?"

"Convention."

"The Fruit Loops are okay."

"Oh, we're not eating in this dive, ha! I won't say anything about ... well, about this. Michael-David, I knew you were different the minute I met you. It's just that you have such a strange way of doing things."

"Thanks."

"Not different in the good way. Wait, that didn't come out right. But you'll be okay."

She smiles at me. I think it's pity. Maybe I've lost weight and look terrible. I'm pretty sure I haven't brushed my teeth in days. My breath might smell like ass. Or maybe she knows exactly what I'm running from and why. In a different life, Diane and I could be good friends. She knows how to push all of my buttons, except for the ones that immobilize me.

"But I'd stay away from Chris," she says.

"Why?"

Diane sits me down in the lobby. Two plush occasional chairs. She tells me everything. I can't believe how much I got right, and how much I got wrong. It's both too pompous and too embarrassing to say. But I can reveal that whatever cruel human trait I've spun, whatever base and cowardly act, whatever lie and act of self-protection, it's all confirmed. But so are the impossible acts of love that I thought were just fairy tale, too fantastical to believe. Then she says something strange, very strange, and leaves it half-explained. She gets up, gives me a kiss on the lips, and walks off. I am dumbfounded by every aspect of our exchange.

"Diane? Diane, what do you mean?"

Nothing but the back of her head. I can't believe she's pulling this on me again. Making me wonder in the wake of her silence. She's just trying to torture me. Maybe it's flirting.

I remember Chris's GPS. What the GPS imagined about me and Diane. Right here. Only now, Diane is gone. But I feel no terror. Only the sure footing of what must happen. I don't know if I'm still telling the story, or just watching it unfold. I have never really known the difference.

Chris fucking Culpepper himself has just walked in through the revolving doors. He sees me immediately. He looks agitated, his face redder than I've ever seen it. I think he's hammered.

"Hey, asshole, thought you could hide from me? Ha!"

I say nothing.

"Where is she?"

"Who?"

"Don't play that game. I just saw you two making out. How long have you been fucking Diane?"

"You're insane."

"I bet she blows you like a little slut, doesn't she? She sucks that fat cock of yours and you make her say your name, but she can't because she's choking on it. Am I right, you gutless bastard? You couldn't wait until we broke up. You couldn't get a fucking escort, you rich piece of shit? Had to steal my girlfriend."

It gives me a charge to know I was right about the cuckolding stuff.

"What do you have to say about ruining my career?" I ask.

"I could ask you the same thing. We had a chance at making a great movie together. A fantastic one. But you ruined it. I came here to get you so we could do some publicity, but it's not worth it anymore. I've watched the movie again and again, and I'm certain it's a piece of shit. You know why? Because *you're in it*."

"I want a fucking apology," I say.

"You're not getting one."

"I deserve it!"

"Deserve. That's hilarious. You're the most self-entitled piece of shit I've ever met, you know that?

Now, if I were RR and not me, I would probably shoot him at this point.

That's when I see Tim in the lobby. He can see I'm in trouble, and he knows what to do. At least that's what the reassuring smirk on his face tells me, that he can handle the situation better than I can. That's the thing. While I've been hiding in this hotel, with a fake sense of security but ultimately defenceless, Tim has been on the alert, looking out for himself and for me, always six steps ahead. Now he sidles up to me. I decide to give him a little more information, because it could help us both.

"Hey, puppy," I say to him. "Careful your new friend here doesn't cut off your ears. He's a bad farmer. He's the one who's been giving the puppy very bad dreams."

"Yeah, I smelled him from across the street."

Chris looks confused. Of course, Tim has probably been waiting for him all along, cowering in the corner of the barn, growing his taste for revenge. That's the thing about a recurring nightmare. Every time it tiptoes into your head, you can anticipate the horror a little better. You know what's going to happen. By the time Chris got here, Tim probably knew the exact time, what he would be wearing, how strongly he would reek of alcohol, his exact degree of pitifulness. A perfect profile refined through the memory of dreams, the algorithms that run them. Once again, it's math. Tim would most certainly know how Chris would die. A consummate scientist, he wouldn't let a detail that important escape him, not my Tim.

"Does one of you psychos have a cigarette?" Chris asked.

Tim pulls a pack out of his jeans pocket.

"Fuck, yeah. Thanks," says Chris.

Tim flips the box open and runs his index along the tips of the cigarettes. The finger stops. He pulls a particular cigarette out, gives it to Chris, and lights it for him.

Chris takes a long deep draw and exhales. I finally get it. He takes another drag, and I enjoy the moment. Tim and I watch it happen. Chris's body goes numb one limb at a time. His left arm is the first to wilt. It flaps helplessly, and we watch him panic as he tries to make it move, and soon his face starts to morph. Blue tinge creeping from slight to severe. I can't help but think about the woolly mammoths who were paralyzed this way, frozen in time in the middle of Los Angeles. He looks up at me with frantic eyes, and I think of something to say to him, something that will paint his last few seconds of life so vividly that he will die in an explosion of colour. What I tell him is both loving and heartless. It is the last thing he wants to hear. It will indeed be the last thing, and it will give him such a boner.

"Diane told me that she fucked Spike Jonze and kept the condom. You drank a little bit of him for breakfast every day for a week."

The look, the look.

Chris collapses on the floor and twitches a few last stabs at life. Smoking kills, so there will always be a fatal puff. Nicotine overdose is mean to him indeed. I can see a huge erection bulging through his jeans.

We have a lobby full of witnesses and I don't give a fuck.

Tim and I cab to the La Brea Tar Pits, where we drink beer and toss the empties into the muck, awaiting the resurrection of the wolves. We predict how it will happen: the ancient bones will rise through the tar, rattling and sticky, and start to reassemble, wolf part by wolf part, a swirl of silver-tipped fur and loose, chattering teeth, descending lightly on the grass as whole organisms, but with stomachs empty and in dire need of food.

They will be starving, and they will look at us.

ABOUT THE AUTHOR

DANIEL ALLEN COX is the author of the novels *Shuck* and *Krakow Melt*, which have been shortlisted for the ReLit Awards, the Lambda Literary Awards, and a Ferro-Grumley Award for LGBT Fiction. *Krakow Melt* will soon be published in Turkish as part of an underground literature series. Daniel lives in Montreal.